- For N.E. Elementary's 2015-2016 3rd Grade Class -
..especially Cam,
who showed me that with hard work and a good sense of humor
we can accomplish just about anything
(even fractions)

Jeans

HALO CAT

Lexi

so happy am i to get to call you my friend. you are such a genuine human, a rose quartz of humans i'd even say. you've been here for me in any way i could ever even think to ask. Thank you lex. i love you and hope to always share in your life in some way. You are so powerful Alexis Anderson.

love julia

Jens

HALO CAT

Dear,

So happy am I to get to
call you my friend. You are
such a genuine human,
a rare $ware of human and
I'd ever say. You're been
here for me in any way
I could ever, ever think
to ask. Thank you for it. I love
you and hope to always
be here in your life in
same way. You are so powerful
Glas Anderson.
Love Julia

Prologue
- A Curious Cat Resides Here -

    To the doctors and nurses working on the 7th floor pediatric ward of Piedmont Hospital, Desmond was, for the most part, your typical cat. He enjoyed sunning himself on the children's beds. He was notorious for batting around forgotten surgery masks that had fallen to the floor, and for weaving between the staff's legs as they walked. He was very much a cat in that his feline pride was easily hurt, and as the offender you could count on Desmond letting you know you did wrong by watching him watch you from half-closed eyes while twitching his tail in your direction.

    But like a cat, he badly wanted your attention, so he would never stay mad long, in case he missed out on a good chin scratch. Desmond slept on a bed of three blankets that had been plucked out of the lost and found when Dr. Clement first brought him up to the 7th floor. His bed was tucked under a corner of the nurse's station so he could sleep peacefully without fear of his tail being stepped on. However, it was rare to find his magnificent silver body curled up there under the desk. When looking for Desmond, you had a better chance of finding him by poking your head into the patients' rooms one by one. There you would often find him sharing a bed with the child that occupied it, snuggled at their feet or their shoulder, or sometimes purring away lazily on their stomachs.

    In these ways, Desmond was your average everyday feline, but there were also a couple curious things about him. For one, he seemed to understand when someone would talk to him, or even about him - especially if it wasn't very nice. It was also peculiar the way the children would talk to Desmond as if he were a real person. On more than one occasion, a nurse had walked into a child's room and heard the patient asking Desmond a question as if they expected he would answer them back!

Another thing that made Desmond interesting was his thick glossy coat that shone like leaves turned silver in the moonlight. Even in the darkest of rooms a hazy glow seemed to hang around him like a halo. To add to his curious appearance, eight evenly spaced rings marched from the base of his tail up almost to its tip. All eight rings were wrapped around Desmond's tail like smoky gray halos.

Regardless of his peculiarities, the 7th floor pediatric staff regarded Desmond as a great addition to their work family. Desmond, having been brought to the floor roughly three years before, remained as the resident therapy animal.

It was this role that Desmond took very seriously. He was a comfort to many a child that stayed on the floor, and since the doctors and nurses regarded Desmond as a lovable and respected oddity, they were grateful for the happiness and comfort he provided the children.

But for the children, Desmond was much more. He was the strangest yet kindest, most wonderful thing they had ever known. Each child that spent a night on the seventh floor was sure to find out why.

Chapter 1
- Cat-In-A-Box -
(Summer - July 1994)

Desmond did not always live on the 7th floor of Piedmont Pediatric Hospital, though he had little more than fuzzy, confusing images of his home before the ward. Six years ago, Desmond had been the ninth kitten born into a family who had enough trouble trying to feed their own children, let alone nine more cats. Therefore, his owner sat beside pump #3 at Flash Gas with a cardboard box full of sleeping kittens. Every once in a while, someone would stop to peer into the box and admire the fluffy bodies all huddled in one corner, but no one wanted to take one home.

A woman wearing a t-shirt that read "Crazy Cat Lady" looked longingly at the cats, but ran away muttering "Bert says he'll go on leavin' and stay at his brother's house if I bring another one home." At the same time Dr. Clement was walking down the street on his way to work thinking about how he was going to watch Dr. Weston perform an especially difficult surgery on the Bryant boy later that afternoon. He had started to think so fondly about the adorable way Dr. Weston hummed while she operated, that he almost didn't notice the man nodding off in the sun beside a large box.

I believe I recognize him...

Dr. Clement believed the man called himself Jeb Maycomb. If he was correct he knew that Mr. Maycomb was known around town as a man down on his luck.

He thought that he might be begging - a quite unusual activity for such a proud man, but nonetheless Dr. Clement reached for his pocket. Surprisingly enough, when he leaned over and peeked inside the box, he did not see coins and loose bills as he had expected. Instead, he saw a number of multicolored kittens. Dr. Clement ran his short fingers through his long mustache.

Hadn't he and Dr. Weston just read an article on all the good things animals can do for sick patients?

Why yes, he believed they had.

Perhaps if he were to bring one of these kittens to the hospital, he or she could live there year-round and keep the children company.

Yes, he thought, *and maybe Dr. Weston will be impressed by my sensitivity and thoughtfulness*.

"Sir," he said gruffly, startling the man with the box awake. His bottom lip bulged fat with chewing tobacco, a nasty habit some men never gave up. "Could you tell me how much these kittens are, please?"

The man rubbed his eyes before grunting "free, if you have a good home to bring 'em back to."

Dr. Clement's fingers twitched in his pocket; he loved a good deal and was rather disappointed that the cats cost nothing because he loved to haggle. But he supposed that free was a better deal than even he could work, and consented to bending down to get a better look.

Immediately, one kitten caught his eye. He was silvery-gray, and had a fuzzy looking glow about him.

"Say!" said Dr. Clement as he scooped up the kitten, "this guy here, he looks just like that anchor on the six o'clock news. What's his name… Desmond Weatherby?"

Dr. Clement chuckled and held the kitten up to his face.

"Same silvery hair and no-nonsense expression, eh?"

The man grunted in agreement and moved the box out of the sun.

"He's a funny one, that'un is," said the man. "All the other kittens always go to where he is, kinda like they feel good or somethin' when they're near him. Right beauty, too. I never seen a cat that color before. I'm surprised you ain't got more competition on trying to bring him home."

"Sometimes, the most wonderful things are hidden in plain sight, right before our eyes," said Dr. Clement, thinking himself clever enough to see the potential of the silver kitten.

"Even so, he's mighty peculiar. You see those rings, Doc? When he was born, he had them there rings on his tail, even though it was no bigger than my pinky finger," he waggled his little finger at Dr. Clement to show him just how tiny the kitten's tail had been at birth.

"Yep, had nine of 'em at first, though. Top one at the tip faded 'bout a week after they were born. Dunno why, but there yeh have it. So you want him or no?"

"Seems like a fine fella to me. Here you are," Dr. Clement offered the man a crisp $5 bill.

"No sir, not asking any money for 'em. Just tryna find 'em some good homes."

Dr. Clement noticed a hole in the tip of the man's shoe and said, "well, I figure I just nabbed the best looking puss in your box. I'd feel mighty wrong if I went on taking him without giving you anything in return, seeing as how fine a feline he truly is."

The man still didn't take the money Dr. Clement held in his outstretched hand.

"Tell you what," said the doctor giving up and pocketing the bill. "Your youngest girl, does she still have that cough?"

"Yessir, I reckon she does."

"Bring her by day after next and I'll get her checked out and sent home with some medicine. How's that sound?"

"I don't accept charity, Doc. Surely you understand that."

"Not charity, just a trade. I can't feel right about leaving you with nothing while I walk away with a brand spankin' new kitten! Surely you can understand that."

"Yea, I reckon I do. I'll bring her by 'round… 3 o'clock?"

"Mr. Maycomb, you've got yourself a deal."

Dr. Clement smiled and made to walk away and continue on his route to work, but he hesitated.

"By the way, I had a cousin who liked to chew dip," the doctor added, pointing to the man's puffy lower lip. "Lost half his tongue cause of the stuff."

Surprisingly, the man's face broke into a toothy grin. "Just chewing gum, Doc. Quit the hard stuff when my oldest was born - just miss the feeling really. He pulled out a wad of gray gum as proof before placing it back between his gum and bottom lip.

And just like that, the special silver kitten became Desmond, resident cat on the 7th floor of Piedmont Hospital.

Chapter 2

- Special Delivery -

(Summer - July 1994)

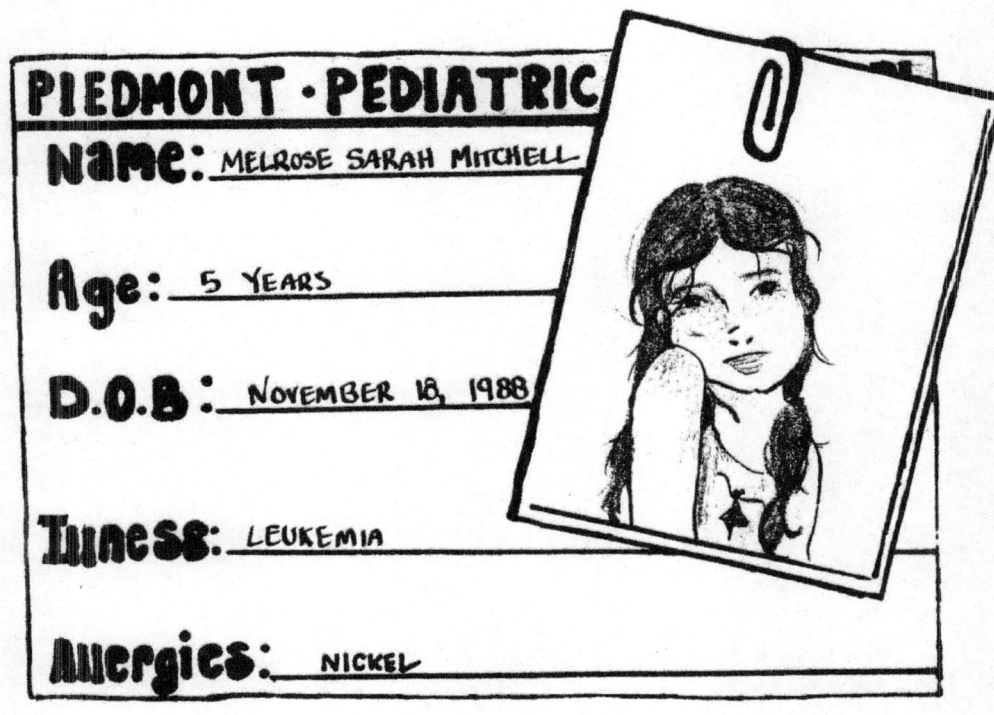

The little kitten bounced around in Dr. Clement's pocket. He let out a few croaky meows as his paws slid down the steep sides of his confine. Just a few minutes ago he had been snoozing peacefully among his brothers and sisters. Then, while dreaming of the taste of warm milk, he had been plucked rudely out of his box, thrust into dazzling sunlight, and then deposited in a jacket pocket.

The kitten tensed and crouched. He could hear many busy noises coming from the opening above his head.

Honk! Honk! yelled a car.

"Safe to walk now, sir," advised a crossing guard.

"Howdy, Doc!" called a gentleman's voice.

"Mornin', Vern. Make sure Lucy keeps that foot elevated, you hear? And no more backflips off the back porch, the little daredevil," Dr. Clement's laughter rumbled like thunder.

The kitten couldn't get out and so he laid down in the crease of the pocket and waited to find out where he'd end up next.

After several more minutes, Dr. Clement walked through the doors to Piedmont Hospital. He waited, grinning under his mustache as the elevator carried him up to the seventh floor.

Ding!

Dr. Clement stepped out and scanned right and then left for Dr. Weston. With a leap of his heart, he spotted her by the nurses' station bent over a clipboard.

"Good morning, Bonnie," said Dr. Clement in what he thought was his most charming voice.

"Oh, hello Eugene," started Dr. Weston and she blushed, stealing glances at Dr. Clement from under her eyelashes.

"Call me Gene," Dr. Clement said perhaps a tad too eagerly, for he quickly added, "if you want to, of course," and this time it was Dr. Clement who turned pink.

"Alright then, I'll know for next time," said Dr. Weston as she smiled and brushed fly-away gray hair out of her eyes.

Dr. Clement seemed to suddenly remember why he had sought her out in the first place. Pulling the kitten out of his pocket, the doctor explained how he had been inspired by his discussion with Dr. Weston the previous week on pet therapy. Hadn't she told him of new research that studied the benefits that animals had on people's health and happiness?

"Why, I did," Dr. Weston said breathlessly and she held the kitten under her chin and scratched behind his ears.

"Decided to name him Desmond after the weatherman on channel 10. I reckon this cat's got that same silvery color as his hair," Dr. Clement rocked on his heels.

"Well, I reckon he does indeed," gushed Dr. Weston. "That's a mighty fine name for a mighty fine puss... Gene."

Dr. Clement seemed to swell with pride. He puffed out his chest and mumbled something that sounded like "snuffin."

"Oh, he's shaking, the poor angel," Dr. Weston hugged the kitten closer.

"What do you say about putting him in Melrose Mitchell's room for a bit? I hear she's been having trouble sleeping at night."

"Oh, that's a wonderful idea. Mel Mitchell is just darling. She and Desmond will be best friends before you can say 'Frannie finds felines fabulously fun!'"

Desmond was cradled down the hall and placed in a bed next to a little girl. She didn't wake up when he stumbled onto her chest and curled up in the hollow of her collarbone.

Several hours later, the kitten woke himself up by calling out to his brothers and sisters in his dream. His heart hammered against his rib cage and his body shook in tiny spasms.

"Did you say something?" came a small voice from very close.

Two blue eyes studied Desmond from above. They belonged to the little girl who shared her bed with him. Desmond croaked out that he was thirsty and scared.

The child stared at him a moment longer before taking a full cup of water from the bedside table. She offered it to the kitten and asked if she could pet him. He gave a hum of approval and began lapping up the water.

"I wouldn't usually ask," began the girl as she stroked Desmond's back, "but then again, I wouldn't normally expect a kitty to answer even if I did." Desmond wasn't quite sure what she meant but he started to purr when her fingers rubbed the silky fuzz behind his ears. He drank until he could feel the water sloshing around inside his belly.

"Who are you?" Desmond purred, now feeling relaxed and comforted by the girl's warm hand.

"Mel. Wha' 'bout you?"

Desmond faintly remembered strange voices remarking how me made for a very handsome 'Desmond.'

"Desmond, I think, but I've never heard of a Desmond before."

"Well, I've only ever heard of two Desmonds in my life," said Mel as she leaned back against her pillow. "There's Desmond Edgar; he writes poems that my daddy reads to me. And then there's Desmond Weatherby on channel 10 news, but my mom says 'he's full of more hot air than the giant heatwave he forecast on his first day.' Whatever that means."

Desmond yawned, revealing a half dozen or so sharp white teeth. Mel watched the kitten press his paws into her shoulder. She closed her eyes for a bit and just listened to his purring.

"I won't tell them you can talk," Mel said with her eyes still closed. For the second time since he'd met Mel, Desmond wasn't sure what the little girl meant. Who wouldn't she tell? And what was she not going to tell them, again? This peculiar creature made Desmond el very safe, even though she wasn't completely covered in fur, save for the top of her head. She was very warm and smelled like dried flowers in autumn.

    Desmond felt safe enough to climb onto her chest and ride the slow rising and falling of her breath. He reached out his nose and touched it to Mel's lip. Slowly and ever so gently Mel reached up her hands and cupped Desmond's small head. She leaned forward and gave him several short, quick kisses in the dip between his eyes. Then, she placed one hand on his back towards his rear and the tiny kitten purred like a small engine. Mel could feel him vibrating all the way up her arm into her elbow. Within minutes, both had fallen asleep neither knowing that each would change the other's life forever.

Chapter 3

- Tuna For Me and a Hat For You -

(Fall - November 1994)

"Desi, cut it out," Mel giggled.

With exceptional skill Desmond managed to hook his claws into the ball of yarn right before it rolled off the edge of the bed.

"C'mon Melrose, you know this is too much fun to pass up," said Desmond, rolling onto his back. He hugged the yarn to his chest with his front paws and proceeded to kick it with his back legs. Mel tried to work the wriggling yarn with her delicate fingers.

"Nana says that hats are the best thing to knit. She says "you can never have enough hats Melrose Sarah Mitchell. Especially for those ears of yours," Mel made her voice all rough and croaky like her Nana's and tucked a lock of hair behind her ear. Mel's ears stuck out like a pair of half-moons from the sides of her head.

"Jonas says my ears stick out so far they have their own orbit."

Desmond looked over to see Mel frowning at her knitting needles. Sometimes he thought he would never understand Melrose; his ears stuck straight up and out of the top of his head. He had always considered them some mighty fine ears - they were great for hearing small sounds and even made him seem a couple inches taller.

"My ears stick out," said Desmond, "and you tell me all the time how I'm such a pretty kitty.' Besides, you have very special ears. Yours are the only ears that work properly. No one else can hear me."

Mel thought about this for a moment. She must have decided that her ears couldn't be all bad because she allowed a smile to play on her lips.

It was true: Mel was the only human who could hear Desmond. Not long after arriving, he realized that a talking cat was not something you saw everyday - or ever, really. So, Desmond had decided to test if anyone besides Mel could hear him.

He had been sitting at the nurse's station across from Dean with his eyes half closed and thudding his tail against the counter (so everyone would know he was bored) when Dr. Elle Quentin walked up.

"Hey, Elle," Dean the nurse started, "a couple of us are picking up dinner from down the street. You want anything?"

"Ugh, that'd be great, Dean. It's been a long day - started with the 15 year old in room 702 trying to take his IV out. I haven't eaten since then and I desperately need a break," Dr. Quentin sighed and leaned against the counter. She looked like if it weren't there, she would topple right over.

"Do they have cheesesteaks?"

"Yea, chicken or steak, up to you."

"Steak, please, with… fried onions, extra cheese, ketchup, and double extra pickles."

"And I'll take a can of their best tuna," Desmond added, stretching his arms and flexing his claws. "Preferably white chunk, if they have it."

Desmond looked at Dr. Quentin and Dean expectantly.

"Cheesesteak with fried onions, extra cheese, ketchup and extra extra pickles," Dean recited as he copied her order onto a scrap of paper.

"Ahem... And my tuna, let's not forget. And please do see if they have any green olives to put on top. They add such great flavor."

Again, it was as if Desmond hadn't spoken.

"You're truly amazing Dean, a life saver. Thank you," Dr. Quentin handed Dean some money before turning to walk away.

"Oh, hey Des. Didn't see you there," she worked her hand from his head all the way down to his rear and followed the length of his tail. "Such a beautiful cat," she said to herself as she hurried down the hall. Desmond had a feeling she was headed to room 702 to make sure the boy in there hadn't pulled his IV out since the last time she'd checked.

Ever since then, Desmond had known that only Melrose could hear him. This information bothered Desmond very little - he didn't care that no one else could understand him. Mel could, and that was all that mattered.

By now Desmond had been calling the 7th floor his home for a little over 6 months. Melrose was there the whole time, and Desmond was rarely found anywhere but on her bed. Only when Desmond ate, used the litter box, and was kicked out of Mel's room so the doctors could poke and prod her, could he be seen in other places throughout the ward.

Naturally, the two had become inseparable. Desmond would sit for hours while Mel drew or painted. He would bat at her pencil while she worked, sometimes pushing it off course and changing the image. But Mel never erased when this happened. Instead, when the picture was finished she would sign her name and Desmond's, saying that they had made it together.

Since Mel spent most of her time stuck in bed making pictures, it wasn't long before she had more stacks of finished artwork than enough table space to keep them. Desmond had the idea to hang them up on the walls and around her bed - she did and sometimes the two would sit and admire the pictures, thinking of the afternoons they had spent making them.

But it wasn't all great. Melrose was, after all, a patient in the hospital. She had something that Des had heard the doctors refer to as Leukemia, though it sounded much different than it was spelled.

"Loo - keem - ee - uh," Mel advised him in the beginning of their friendship. "It means my blood is very sick, and since there's blood in my whole body, it makes it very hard for me to get better."

What Leukemia meant to the doctors was that this little girl must be subjected to multiple rounds of something called chemotherapy and radiation. Desmond wasn't sure why she had to do this, or why it was considered medicine since it only seemed to make her feel worse whenever she had a treatment. It made all of her soft red hair fall out, even her eyebrows and eyelashes.

So, Mel's nana decided to come and show her how to knit on her birthday. This way, Melrose could keep busy while also making hats to keep her head warm.

"When I was six I learned how to knit, sew, and cook. I figure you've got more than enough time to learn at least one of those things, Melrose."

Mel's tiny fingers became sore and red as she practiced her knitting. Sometimes Desmond would try to persuade her to take a break and give her fingers a rest. He did this even though batting around Mel's yarn ball while she worked was his favorite game.

The two friends couldn't imagine the hospital, or life, for that matter, to be the same without the other. Each entered the hospital scared and lonely, but had fortunately soon found each other. Melrose loved Desmond as much as her little heart could. His nights spent purring at her side seemed to fill her with a renewed strength of some sorts. In the months they spent together, Mel's laugh became louder - it swelled inside your very chest, reached down deep into you, and pulled your own laughter out. She spent more time alert and coloring than sleeping. This pleased the nurses who lavished Mel with flowers they picked on their way to the hospital, beautiful new crayons, and silk ribbons, now that Mel's hair was growing back again.

When no one else was in the room, Desmond and Mel would talk. They'd talk for hours if uninterrupted. When Mel couldn't sleep because of her treatments, Desmond would listen intently about Mel's rabbit that she kept at home, her teacher and friends at school, and her favorite topic: the week she spent at art camp.

Yes, Desmond and Melrose had found in each other the friend of a lifetime. The doctors and nurses remarked at how devoted a kitten that was plucked from a box outside could be to a child. They smiled and shook their heads when they saw Desmond waiting patiently outside Mel's door until the doctor would let him back in. But mixed with their smiles and amusement of the curious relationship was a splash of fear and a pinch of worry.

For they wondered what would happen if the pair was ever separated for any reason, and they feared they would have to find out much too soon.

Chapter 4
- A Lightbulb That Grew Whiskers -
(Winter - February 1995)

It was a dreary kind of day. The clouds outside Mel's window imitated the dark gray of the eight smoky rings on Desmond's tail with one exception: the clouds were like a grimy dime compared to the shine of the cat's coat.

Desmond was half asleep purring alongside the drumming of raindrops when he heard Mel speak.

"Des, I wanna draw you," her voice was tiny, as if she were across the room and not on the bed next to him.

"Why do you want to do that, Mel?" Desmond said without opening his eyes. He was trying to buy himself a few more moments to stay curled up (Desmond loved lazy rainy days - he got to appreciate staying dry and warm while the world outside got wet).

"Because you're glowing, Desi, like you have a halo all around you."

Desmond opened his eyes this time, but only a bit. He could see his paws from the position he was laying and didn't notice anything particularly unusual. Mel reached out a hand, and cupping his chin in her fingers, she rubbed his forehead with her thumb. Desmond's purring grew louder.

At last he sighed. Mel knew how to soften up the hardest of folk.

"How do you want me to pose?" Desmond asked in mock defeat.

"Just stay where you are," said Mel. "You don't have to do anything special." She gave him a final chin scratch and then turned to pick up her water color set and a piece of clean paper. Desmond watched her out of the corner of one open eye. His whiskers stretched back in a grin as Mel dipped her brush in her drinking glass and got to work.

Drip Drop Drippity Drip

The rain outside Mel's window beat steadily against the glass. It sounded like the trot of hundreds of horses pounding away at the earth. Every now and then when the rain would take a break, the heavy clouds, bloated with water, would move aside and the moon would peek out from behind them, reminding the world "I'm still here!"

That night, the moon was a small sliver, a pearly crescent that hung like a lopsided smile among the stars. Desmond and Melrose had fallen asleep several hours earlier and the entire floor was quiet.

When it was dark in the hospital, the noises were different. Although, the loud laughter and bickering of siblings and friends come to visit were silenced, the beeping machines still played their endless monotone tune. Occasionally, you might here an abrupt cough or the soft sweeping footsteps of the night nurse checking to make sure his or her patients were resting peacefully. The doctor's booming voices that called out orders now rested with their owners.

That night the rain added to the usual after-dark soundtrack of the hospital. Strangely enough, the drumming of rain seemed to make the floor even quieter somehow. It brought an eerie sleepiness to the Piedmont Pediatric Ward. Even the night nurse found herself nodding off at her seat behind the desk and several times she woke herself up when a sudden snore escaped from the back of her throat.

An itch on Desmond's neck tore him from a deep sleep. He kicked it with the claws on his back leg - several swift swipes and the itch was gone.

Desmond yawned. His sharp white teeth parted and his rough pink tongue curled back just outside of his jaws. His orb-like eyes scanned the room. He could feel Mel's slow and steady breathing beside him and knew she was still asleep.

With an almighty stretch, Desmond stood up. He twitched his tail without really thinking about it and studied the numbers and squiggly lines that zigzagged across the screens of Mel's machines. Everything seemed normal to Desmond. The numbers he saw were a little lower than they'd been, but nowhere near the range that caused the machines to start screaming and several nurses to run panic-stricken into the room.

Still, *something just doesn't feel right*, thought the cat.

Desmond turned his head to look at Melrose, who looked pretty much the same as always.

Perhaps a bit paler than usual, he thought. But her lips were still quite pink and her breathing was even.

Yet the fur at the base of Desmond's tail wasn't lying flat like it normally did.

Then suddenly, as if it happened because Desmond was waiting for something to happen, Mel choked on the breath she was taking.

Desmond's heart jumped into his throat and his tongue went dry.

He pressed his paw to her chest and a great shuddering breath shook her whole itty bitty body. Then, she coughed, just once, and returned to deep sleepy breathing.

Desmond twitched his right whiskers, then his left. His whole body felt cold yet electrified. He looked back at the monitors with their blinking red dots and acid green lines that carved sharp mountains and low valleys across the screen.

"Des," croaked Mel. With a start, Desmond's head snapped around to face her.

"Mel… you should be sleeping," the cat tried to sound disapproving to hide the fact that his voice was shaking. The truth was, Desmond had just experience the most terrifying moment of his life, though seeing Mel awake allowed Desmond's to heart settle in his chest like an old man lowering himself uncertainly into a seat.

Desmond walked over to her, pretending he hadn't been staring at her monitors. He brushed the tip of his tail under her chin once, twice, three times as he spun in a circle before he lay down.

Mel laughed because it tickled, but only air came out, not her thick, tinkling laughter that hugged a person's heart.

"*You're* awake," Mel argued, doing a terrible job of hiding her fragile smile.

"And *you're* just as stubborn in the middle of the night as you are during the day."

Mel narrowed her eyes and wrinkled her nose like she was offended, but in the end she couldn't hold it inside - a grin spread across her face revealing a missing front tooth.

Desmond did a better job of hiding his own smile by becoming very interested in biting an itch on his left paw.

"Des," Mel said again with more urgency this time.

The force with which Melrose said his name made Desmond pause. He raised his light eyes to hers, letting her know she had his attention.

"Is it true that cats have nine lives?"

"I thought you didn't believe in stuff like that." He lowered his paw back to the bed. Having such a serious illness at such a young age made it hard for Mel to believe in magic. She spent every day in the most un-magical of situations, watching doctors tell her parents scary things that made them sad and turn an ugly grayish color over time.

"I didn't used to, ever since I can remember, but I didn't used to believe in talking cats either."

"Fair enough. As far as I know, it's just an old wives tale, but what made you wonder that?"

"Well, I was dreaming it just before I woke up. I was dreaming that I was here, in the hospital, but it wasn't this room." Mel frowned. "You were there, but you weren't you, Desmond. You had a different shape… you were a light bulb."

"I was a - what?"

"A light bulb. You were up above my head and you still had whiskers - that's how I knew it was you in my dream."

"A light bulb, of course…. maybe we should have skipped that pudding before bed," teased Desmond.

"No, Desi. It wasn't a bad dream, it was good, or it felt good anyway. But it didn't make sense, because you told me that you had lots of light and because I was down where it was dark, you would shine some of your light on me and..."

"And what, Mel?"

"And it would make me all better," she whispered, her voice trailing off as she dropped her eyes.

Desmond studied the little girl's face until his eyes stung. He didn't realize he had forgotten to blink.

"I thought you said the dream felt happy, or good, at least," said Desmond.

"It did," Mel muttered.

"Then why do you seem sad?"

"Because it was just a dream - I had to wake up."

And that's when Desmond understood. For the span of several seconds Mel had felt a small seed of hope be planted inside her brave heart. As quickly as it had been planted, before it could grow roots and bloom, it had been ripped out. Once Mel opened her eyes and remembered where she was, the magic had disappeared. She came crashing down from a world where she could be free of beeping machines, needles, and painful treatments, only to find herself surrounded by them once again. As good as the dream felt, waking up to find it wasn't real felt that much worse.

Tears welled in Mel's eyes; she bent her head to rub them away on her shoulder before they could spill down her cheeks.

"Hey," said Desmond standing up again. "Please don't cry Melrose, I'm here."

The cat pressed his forehead against Mel's leaky eyes. Her tears wet his fur but he didn't care.

"I'm scared," she said at last.

"I know. It's okay to be scared."

"Jonas says only babies get scared."

"Well I heard Jonas ask your mom if he could sleep in bed with her and your dad the other day."

"Nah-uh, Jonas is nine, he wouldn't do that," argued Mel stubbornly.

"Yes-huh he would - and he did. It was on Tuesday when visiting hours were ending. I think he misses you. I think he gets scared too, but doesn't want you to know because he's your big brother and he wants you to think he's brave."

Mel considered this. "Jonas says you can't be brave if you're a 'scaredy cat.'"

"I resent that phrase," Desmond said more to himself than to Mel, "but I don't agree. Remember when you were going to have your first radiation treatment?"

"Mm-hmm."

"You were very scared then. Remember you tried to hide under the chair in the corner, but I accidentally gave away your hiding spot."

"You kept trying to play with the strings on my hospital gown!" Mel's eyes sparkled as she pictured a baby Desmond playfully attacking the ties on her dress.

"Yes, I do love a good string, as you know. But my point is that even though you were scared, you still went. That's what being brave means. It doesn't mean you're never scared. It means you try to be brave even though you're scared."

"How do you know?"

"Because, I know. It's a lesson I learned from watching you."

The words hung in the air between them.

"You're plenty brave Melrose, please trust me."

"Okay," and the little girl pulled the cat close to her chest, coaxing out a beautiful deep purr. She stroked his back until they had both fallen back to sleep.

Chapter 5
- Not Even a Goodbye -
(Winter - March 1995)

As Desmond turned the corner he could see the doctors and nurses walking in and out of Mel's room. This wasn't unusual - Mel often had people checking on her throughout the day.

As Desmond got closer, he realized he heard several unfamiliar and very worried voices drifting out of the door. A doctor walked out when Desmond approached the doorway and almost stepped on his paw.

"Sorry, Des. Didn't see ya there," he murmured distractedly and moved to step around the cat, but Desmond, quickly recovering from the almost-offense, simply scampered around the doctor's feet.

He'd only taken one step inside the room before he stopped dead in his tracks.

He twitched his whiskers to the right, then to the left and sniffed the air.

His wide eyes scanned the room and the fur on the base of his tail stood on end.

Something felt different. The air was so thick it got caught in Desmond's throat and it seemed he would choke on it.

None of the adults noticed when he took a few more steps inside.

That was just fine to Desmond. His only thought was for the little girl that lay sleeping on the only bed in the room. The cat jumped up by her feet.

He was cautious and even a bit scared as he approached her face. He touched the tip of his nose to the tip of hers and then rubbed his cheek against against her jaw. She looked so small in the sea of blankets that swallowed her up.

Has she always been this tiny? wondered Desmond.

Mel's lips were pale and cracked and she had wires hooked up to her arms. Desmond sniffed near her eyes and around her ears. He even brushed his whiskers under her chin trying to tickle her awake, but she didn't move.

Something was very wrong.

Mel's breathing was shallow and she hadn't opened her eyes yet or scratched behind Desmond's ears. By now, the cat was trying hard not to panic. As gently as he could, he stepped onto Mel's chest and laid down, purring heavily, but still she did not stir. He head butted her forehead a couple of times. When that didn't wake her, Desmond tried giving her a few light licks under her chin. Desmond's scratchy tongue always made Melrose explode in fits of giggles.

"Desi," she breathed and the cat felt his heart leap in his rib cage.

"Jared! She's awake!" screamed Mel's great aunt on her father's side. "And that cat is trying to crush her! Get him off! She's suffocating!"

Desmond had never looked at a human with such disgust before. How dare she try to say that he would ever hurt Melrose. This was his spot! But before Desmond had a chance to hiss at this stranger like he would have wanted, Dr. Clement walked over and grabbed Desmond around the middle and began pulling him off Mel. Desmond had never known such fear. He let out a low growl, hoping that Dr. Clement would just let go and they would all leave so he could comfort his best friend in peace.

Instead of letting go, Dr. Clement tightened his grip and yanked. Ignoring the pain in his ribs where the doctor's finger tips dug into him, Desmond clung to the sheets with all his might - they got caught in his claws. The fabric stretched and screamed in protest and the strange woman yelled "It's rabid! It's trying to kill the child! Jared!"

At last, the fabric ripped and fell back on Melrose, who still did not open her eyes.

With a soft thud, Desmond was deposited onto the tile floor just outside of Mel's room. He tried to run back in, but Dr. Clement shut the door saying "sorry old boy," just before his face disappeared behind it.

Desmond cried at the door for almost 45 minutes before a nurse came out to try to comfort him. She bent down to run her hand across his back but he sunk low to the ground and hurried closer to the door. Like Dr. Clement, she was too fast - she must have known he might try to run back inside. With a simple click, he was shut out again.

"Mel!" He called out over and again. "Melrose, I'm here!"

No answer came from inside, save for the strange woman's muffled voice wondering what kind of hospital let wild animals run loose around sick children.

Desmond waited outside the door to room 731 all through the night and into the next afternoon. By now, he had stopped trying to run in every time the door opened. It was no use, they knew he was out there so they were extra careful when anyone needed to step outside. Twice Desmond tried hiding behind the nurse's station and sprinting at the door in a surprise attack when he heard it open. It hadn't worked.

He cried "Mel! I'm here! I won't leave you," until he'd lost his voice and no sound escaped him save a tiny croak.

More than a whole day had passed since Desmond had seen Mel; it was the longest he had ever gone. He was hungry and sore and his heart ached. He paced for hours more until a nurse, Dotty, walked up to him with her hands on her hips.

"Desmond, I know you're hungry."

Desmond just stared at her. Food wouldn't help fill the hole that had suddenly dug itself deep into his heart. Dotty walked over and slid her back down along the wall until she was sitting only a couple of feet from where Desmond sat.

Usually Desmond would love to step into Dotty's lap and be stroked and kissed. But right now, he was too heartsick. Dotty seemed to understand.

"You miss your friend," she said, and it wasn't a question. It was a fact.

She reached a hand out and it hung in midair, a few inches from the cat's face. She was telling him she was there if he wanted her, but she wasn't forcing herself on him. While Desmond greatly appreciated that she was giving him the choice, he didn't want Dotty. He only wanted Melrose. But the pain in his chest was getting to be too much and he leaned his head towards Dotty's hand.

Dotty got the hint. She closed the gap between them and stroked the extra silky fur on his chest. Desmond closed his eyes and for several minutes let the comfort of a good pet wash over him. The cat didn't even realize he was purring until Dotty's hand vanished.

"Come eat, Des," she jerked her head towards the nurse's station not far from where they sat. Desmond decided to ignore her and turned back towards the closed door.

"Mel," he called again, silently.

"Okay, I get it," said Dotty as she stood up. Desmond didn't turn around as she left, but once she was gone he felt lonelier than he expected.

The tile floor of the hospital was cold and uninviting. He circled a few times before laying down, resting his chin on his paws.

Desmond sighed.

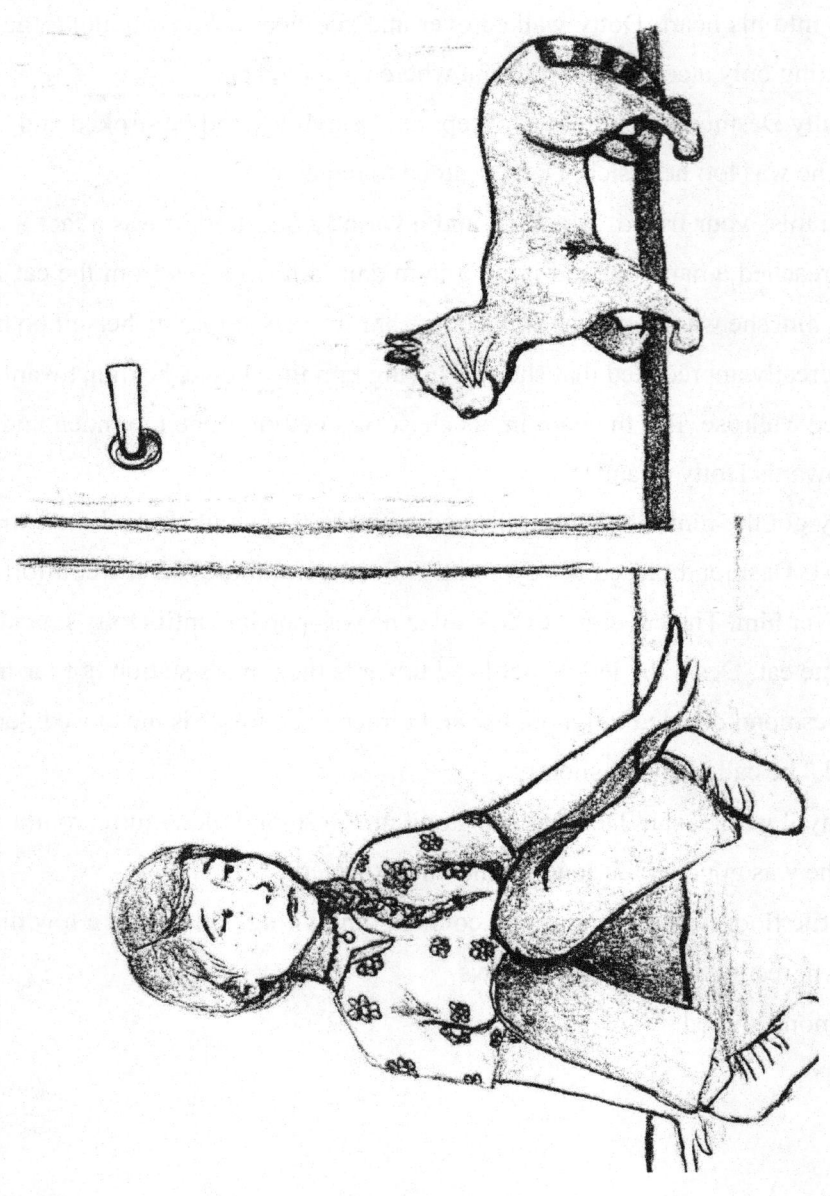

His ears perked up when he heard footsteps down the hall. Dotty was coming back with his bowls and one of his blankets.

"Here you go, you stubborn boy," she said, and she set down his food and water bowl across the hall and arranged the blanket into a very welcoming little nest.

Desmond thanked Dotty by rubbing up against her ankle, but only once for he was still very distressed and heartbroken.

"I'm sorry, Desi," Dotty said and gave him one last scratch behind his ears before walking away back down the hall.

When Dotty was out of sight, Desmond walked over to the food and sniffed it. He couldn't remember ever being so hungry. Checking one last time that Dotty wasn't watching, he gobbled down his first meal in almost two days.

With a full belly, Desmond was suddenly drowsy.

"I'll only close my eyes for a little. A cat nap," he thought to himself and almost smiled in spite of his worried heart.

Desmond lay down in the blankets and curled into a tight ball. He started purring. In less than a minute, he had fallen into a sleep much deeper than a cat nap.

When Desmond woke up it took a moment for him to remember where exactly he was in the hospital. Bright sunlight streamed in through a nearby window. Desmond gave an impressive yawn.

Melrose! he thought and within the same second had already jumped out of the blanket and sprinted the short distance down the hall to room 731.

Ha! Desmond cheered in his head, *they left the door open!* His pink pads slipped a little and his rump flew off to the side, hip-checking the door.

"Melrose! I'm here!" He cried out to an empty room. "Mel?"

The little bed in the center of the room was empty. All the pictures and get-well-cards Mel had hung up so long ago had been stripped from the walls.

Desmond walked very slowly over to the bed. He could still see pieces of tape left on the wall from where Mel had hung the portrait she made of Desmond that rainy afternoon only a week ago - it seemed like a lifetime had gone by since then.

He jumped onto Mel's bed, but it didn't smell like her. It smelled strange and unfamiliar. Desmond sneezed twice.

A nurse came into the room and grabbed the only vase of flowers still on the windowsill.

"Where is she?" Desmond yelled at the woman.

"Oh, Desmond, you scared me," she said as her hand flew to her heart.

The cat just stared back at her, unblinking.

"She's gone Des," the nurse said and she plucked a petal off one of the flowers. "I'm sorry." She looked right in Desmond's eyes as her own filled with tears.

He blinked once and then looked away. The nurse walked out of room 731 and cracked the door. Desmond pressed his paws, one after the other, into the mattress in a kind of rhythmic trance.

Then, he laid down and fell into a fitful sleep full of bad dreams.

Chapter 6

- Ghost Cat -

(Spring - May 1995)

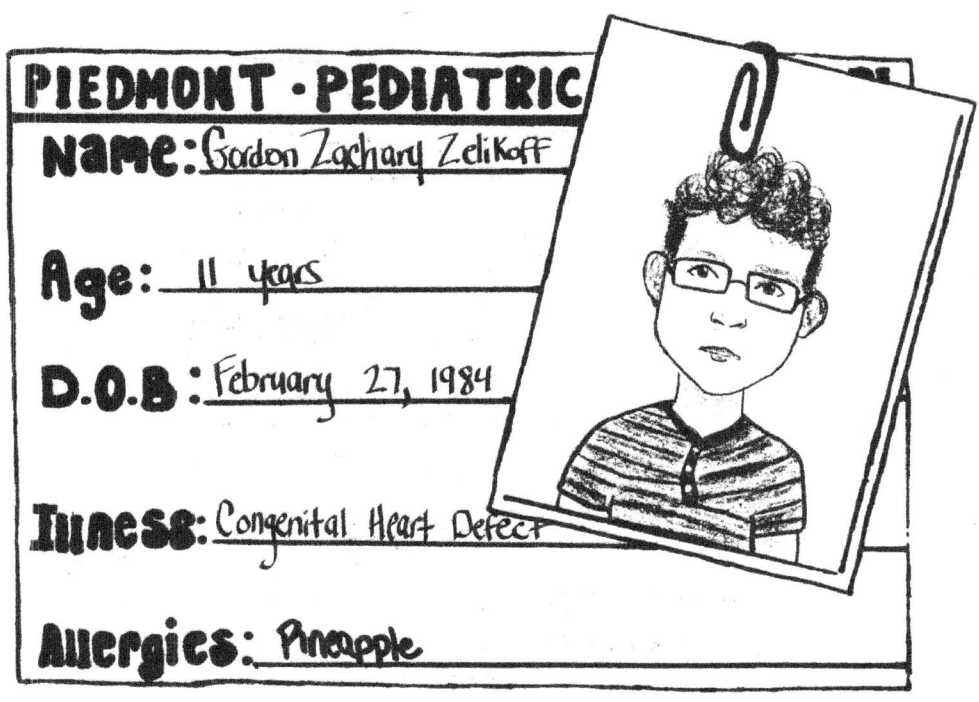

It had been two whole months since Melrose had left the world and Desmond behind. The silver cat's heart still felt shriveled up and hollow.

Several days after Mel died Desmond took up yowling. It disrupted the usual after dark hush and was very bothersome to the nurses that worked overnight. From his loss, Desmond had become more like a ghost than a cat, haunting the halls at night with his sad song.

"Desmond! For the love of jelly donuts, please stop that noise!" a nurse pleaded one night.

Desmond stopped only long enough to fix the nurse with a look that said "I'd like to see you make me."

"Oh Desmond," she said, her voice softening, "you must feel so lonely and confused without your friend. Here you go, kitty kitty," she said and placed one of his favorite salmon flavored treats on the ground at her feet.

But not even the satisfying crunch of a salty snack could fill the hole in Desmond's heart. He neither sniffed the treat nor took a single step towards it.

Instead, he turned around and walked back down the dim hallway, his tail drooping pathetically and dragging behind him on the floor. His low howls bubbled up from the deepest, saddest parts of him. This time, the nurse didn't ask him to be quiet.

Steady.

Shoulders low.

It hasn't seen you yet... And go!

A terrific leap and a small scuffle.

Desmond batted the abandoned surgical mask a couple of times before losing interest.

To the delight of patients and staff alike, Piedmont Pediatric Hospital hadn't had a mouse problem in years. But much to the displeasure of Desmond, the resident therapy cat, this meant his hunting practice was spent pouncing on bits of discarded paper or masks that were forgotten under beds and beside trash bins. It was hard to get much enjoyment from hunting prey that didn't run away, put up a fight, or even move.

What's the point? Desmond thought. He left the crumpled mask behind and walked on to begin a new night spent pacing the halls. Within moments, he had resumed his now familiar yowling.

Back and forth he walked, past the nurses' station and all the dark doorways. He purposefully ignored the dirty looks the night nurse threw his way.

Something strange happened about an hour into Desmond's routine. He noticed that someone else was crying. Had Desmond not understood the pain expressed in a cry like that, he would have been annoyed that someone was interrupting him.

As it were, Desmond had been doing a rather large amount of crying of his own lately, so he was concerned rather than offended. He chose to walk toward the noise.

Since Desmond was a cat, he had better than average night vision. He had no trouble identifying the shaking pile of blankets on the bed in room 717 as the source of the sobbing.

As much as Desmond wanted to back out of the room and return to his own crying, something was pulling him inside.

One paw forward.

Then another.

An invisible magnet drew him closer and closer. The next thing Desmond knew, he was on the bed at the feet of whoever was under the blankets.

"Meow," he said.

The lumpy heap immediately stopped trembling. A mess of unruly blond hair and a pair of dark green eyes glittered in the moonlight. Those eyes studied Desmond, searching him. No doubt this boy had been hearing the cat's haunting howls since his stay began. Slowly, he snaked a hand out from under the blanket and extended it towards Desmond.

Swish Swish

He rubbed his thumb and forefinger together, beckoning Desmond over to him. Now it was Desmond's turn to study the boy. The tears that had spilled from his eyes left glistening trails down his cheeks. They were like the shimmering tracks that snails leave on the sidewalk in the early morning. Desmond blinked once, twice. The boy must have second guessed himself under the silver cat's gaze, because he placed his hand back under the blanket.

Why had Desmond entered the room, jumped up on the bed, and made his presence known if he wasn't even going to let the boy pet him?

Aside from passing children in the hallways, Desmond hadn't been this close to one since Melrose died. Desmond was kind of scared as he looked into Gordon's eyes - they were so different from Mel's. He wanted to jump down and hide under the nurses' station, snuggle down in his blankets and purr himself to sleep.

But then Desmond thought about one of the last nights he spent with Melrose. They had talked about what it meant to be brave. Desmond had told her that being brave was when you tried your best and didn't give up even when you were scared. What kind of cat would Desmond be if he didn't take his own advice? Certainly not a respectable cat. He knew he would never be able to hold his tail up high if he ran away right now just because he was scared.

I am not *a scaredy-cat*, he reassured himself. After such a long pause, the boy was surprised when Desmond took a step closer to him, but never-the-less he stayed very still so as not to spook him and make him run away.

When Desmond got close enough, he could smell the salt that had dried on the boy's cheeks from spilled tears. The cat also smelled something sweet and he spotted a glass of milk still half full on the bedside table. Desmond closed his eyes and began to purr. He was so relaxed, he didn't flinch or open his eyes when the little boy reached his hand out again to stroke his back.

They fell asleep like that, each feeling safer than he had felt in a long time.

Chapter 7
- The Book That Broke the Silence -
(Spring - May 1995)

The boy Desmond had found crying that one night only two short months after Mel's death was named Gordon Zachary Zelikoff. The next morning after they had fallen asleep Desmond woke up from the best night's rest he'd had since Mel. He decided then that he'd be spending more nights in Gordon's room.

Besides, Gordon woke up after an unusually peaceful sleep as well. So why not sleep in his room? He'd forgotten how good it was to be petted and snuggled and sleep up against something warm. So, with this in mind, Desmond went back the next night and the night after that and the night after that. After almost a week of sleeping in room 717, Desmond decided it would probably be beneficial for both him and Gordon if he spent his naps there as well. A short time after that and Desmond was spending the majority of his time sunning himself on Gordon's bed.

Gordon had been staying at the hospital for almost a month. His heart was very sick and couldn't work the way it needed to for the rest of Gordon's body to stay healthy. Not long after he was admitted to Piedmont Pediatric Ward, he had surgery to try to make his heart strong so he'd be free to run, play and just plain old enjoy being a kid. After his surgery, however, Gordon wasn't recovering the way that the doctors had hoped. While the surgery was successful, Gordon wasn't getting any healthier. It was as if the surgery had never happened, except for the fact that the surgery had indeed happened, and as far as the doctors were concerned, should have worked. They didn't know why he wasn't getting any better, so for the time being, they were keeping him in room 717 for observation.

Since Gordon had a heart defect, he wasn't allowed to get up and walk around much. Unfortunately, this was a rule at home as well as the hospital. Often stuck in bed or on the couch, Gordon had learned to pass the time by reading.

His favorite books were fantasy; he loved tales about faraway lands and magic. It was about 4:30 on a Tuesday afternoon when Gordon was re-reading his favorite book out loud to Desmond, who lay across Gordon's knees giving the spaces between his fingers a good cleaning.

"Sissy was no fool. She pulled the stone lever down and in an instant the floor vanished beneath her feet! Luckily, it was just what she had planned. With not a moment's hesitation, Sissy's emerald falcon swooped down and caught her by her backpack in his curved talons. Together, they flew back over the black lake to the mouth of the cave."

Desmond was just thinking to himself how he'd rather be licked by a dog than be carried over a pool of deep black water by a giant bird (the pigeons outside the hospital windows mocked him from the other side of the glass relentlessly) when he realized Gordon had stopped reading.

When Desmond looked up from his bath, he was alarmed to see that Gordon was staring at him with his mouth hanging open and his eyes wide, looking rather alarmed himself!

"D-did... Did you just talk?" he finally managed to splutter out.

Desmond was quiet. Melrose was the only person who could hear him talk. He had tested this theory on some of the staff a while back. Sure enough, they hadn't been able to

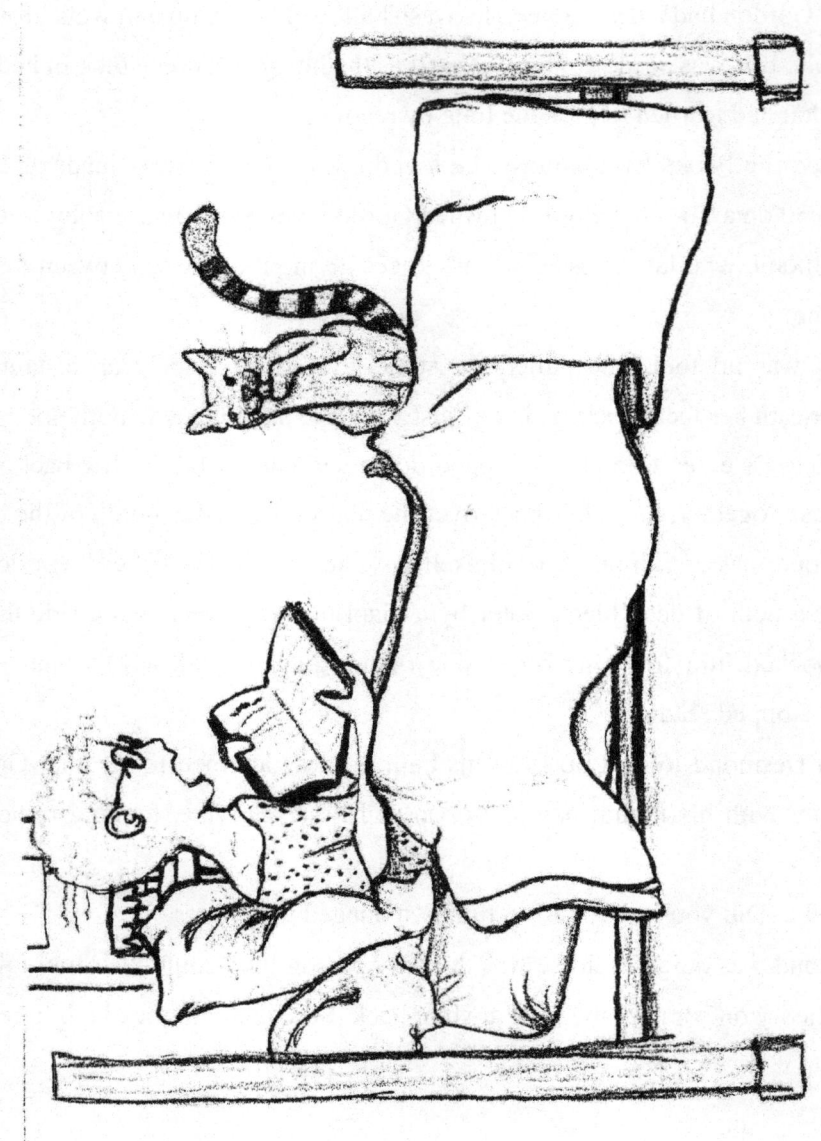

understand him. Then again, he had never tested his theory on another child before - he'd never had any need to. Mel was the only person he had ever really wanted to talk to.

"Maybe?" said Desmond, unsure if Gordon heard him or just someone passing outside the door.

"I'd say that's a bit more than maybe," whispered Gordon.

"Oh, well… then yes. I did, and can - talk. I can talk," Desmond stuttered.

"Have you been able to talk all this time? Or did you just get that power while I was reading?"

"Well, I never thought of it as a power, but I guess I've always had it."

Gordon looked over at his machines as if he was expecting to see the line that went up and down in rhythm his heart beat to spell out "Wake up! You are dreaming!"

But, as it did not say that, Gordon put his hand to his forehead.

"No fever - I can't be hallucinating," he mumbled to himself.

"For someone who loves magic so much, you sure are trying very hard to prove it's fake when it's sitting on your lap."

Desmond was speaking with much more confidence than he felt he truly had at the moment. He had only ever spoken in front of one other person who actually understood him before. In many ways, this was almost as new for Desmond as it was for Gordon.

"Well… how are you doing it then?" the boy pressed.

"I don't know, how are you talking? We just do it, don't we?"

"Yea, but I'm talking because my parents taught me when I was little. I wasn't just born knowing how to talk."

"Then I guess that's why it's magic. Sorry Gordon, but I don't have a better explanation than that."

"Oh… uh, I guess that makes sense then, if it's just magic," Gordon said casually but he looked back over at his heart monitor just to make sure the green lines really hadn't started forming words to tell him he was going crazy.

The pair was quiet for several moments, letting the shock of the situation settle and slowly fade. Once the initial embarrassment had melted away, Gordon began pelting questions at Desmond. They ranged from "why don't cats like water?" to "how's the whole litter-box deal? Good or no?"

Desmond had answered that it was alright, but the best part about it was how cats got to stay nice and dry on rainy days while dogs still had to go outside for their business.

"That's another thing! Why can't cats and dogs get along?"

"Oh they can, and they do. But mostly, it's because of the way dogs beg for their human's attention. All of that rolling over and begging barely leaves any room for a shred of self-respect. We cats are much more dignified and we cringe at the idea of doing tricks for a mere biscuit."

"I knew it!" hissed Gordon, punching his hand with his fist.

"You sure have a lot of questions," remarked Desmond.

"Well it's not every day you meet a talking cat," Gordon pointed out.

"This is true," admitted Desmond, smiling. Desmond was not at all bothered by the dozens of questions Gordon reeled off. In fact, Desmond's cracked, weeping heart was swelling with happiness once again; something he never thought would be possible after seeing Mel's empty bed.

Desmond was talking, and someone lovely was listening.

Chapter 8

A New Beginning

(Spring - June 1995)

Once Desmond realized that Gordon could understand him, life at the hospital became much happier. Over the next couple of weeks Desmond began walking into the rooms of other patients on the floor and introducing himself with an amusingly odd question or statement.

For example, he might say, "did you hear that Dr. Clement cries jelly beans?" or "that tuna looks especially appetizing today. Mind if I steal a bite?"

Desmond felt it would be better if the parents weren't present the first time he introduced himself, even though the adults couldn't hear him. This was a precaution he took very seriously, just in case the kid freaked out - most humans, old or young, had never been asked to share their tuna sandwich with a cat by the cat himself before.

Talking to Gordon had relit the fire in Desmond's heart. As the weeks passed and Desmond's daily visits to Gordon increased in length, several wonderful things happened.

For one, the purple bags that hung like hammocks under Gordon's eyes started to fade. His cheeks began to fill with a rosy color that hadn't been seen for years. Not only were his cheeks filling with color, they were beginning to fill out as well. They were no longer sunken, but showed signs of being round and maybe even chubby in the near future. While this was surely because Gordon's appetite had perked up along with his mood, the doctors and nurses believed Desmond to be the root of these marvelous developments in Gordon's health.

Desmond was also showing signs of a happier life now that he had found Gordon. In the weeks following Mel's death, Desmond had been eating considerably less. He'd been so heartsick that he hadn't had much of an appetite, the result being that he'd become so thin that when he stretched you could see the outlines of his ribs peeking from beneath his sleek fur.

But now, after spending more time with Gordon and the other patients, he was back to his original beautiful self, with the power and energy to chase the nurses' feet and jump onto the tallest counter once again.

Lastly, and much to the over-night nurses' pleasure, Desmond had stopped haunting the hallways at night and instead slept snuggled on Gordon's pillow next to the boy's head. Because Gordon was showing such great signs of improvement, he was set to be discharged from Piedmont by the end of the week.

On the last night of his stay on the 7th floor, Gordon confided his deepest fear in Desmond.

"I've been sick my whole life, Desmond. What if, now that I'm getting better... I'm lousy at all the things other kids do?"

"I'm not sure I understand," Desmond admitted.

"Well, I was never allowed to play sports or run around. My dad always says 'just you wait, Gord-o. Once we get your heart fixed up you can finally play ball. You'll be a natural, just like your old man!'"

"Ahhh, I think I can see where you're going with this now," said the cat.

"Yea, 'cause it was always easy to tell him I couldn't wait to play and make him proud - but that was when I thought I'd never be able to! Now that my heart's getting stronger, he'll want me to be on a team and compete against kids who have probably been playing for years. I've never played before. What if I'm not a natural and I stink? What if I'm a failure and I disappoint my dad?"

"I think there's a more important question here, Gordy."

Gordon's eyebrows drew close together in a frown. He was probably thinking, what could possibly be more important?

"Do you, Gordon, want to play baseball?" Desmond said.

"I think so," Gordon said slowly, carefully. "I think I want to try at least. But I don't wanna disappoint my dad if I'm not fast enough or can't catch the ball. He won the 'Most Valuable Player' award in college twice! Twice, Desmond!" Gordon's voice carried a rising note of panic to the cat's ears and his bottom lip trembled: a tell-tale sign that told him the boy was very near tears.

Desmond thought for a moment about what Gordon was saying. He wanted to answer thoughtfully.

"Gordon, you would say that a fish is a great swimmer, an expert swimmer even?"

"Yea," Gordon had no idea where Desmond was going with this. He knew that the cat's favorite food was tuna, but it seemed an odd time to start discussing fish.

"And you would say that a bird, like say an eagle, is an expert flyer. Yes?"

"Yea," Gordon was openly confused. How had they gone from talking about fathers and football to fish and birds?

"Well, imagine you're a fish, and someone tells you that you have to be a great flyer and start soaring around the clouds. You're probably going to feel lousy when you have trouble getting airborne. And it would be the same thing for a
bird. If you told a bird that it had to dive into deep water and keep up with a fish, it's probably going to feel pretty stupid when it can't. Probably even like a failure."

"Are you saying I'm a fish?"

Desmond laughed, "No Gordon, I'm not saying you're a fish. I'm saying that we all have things that we're especially good at. If we only focus on what we can't do as well as we'd like, we're always going to feel like we're never good enough. A fish who thinks he has to fly to be successful won't ever appreciate his ability to swim. Does that make sense?"

"I think so. Like even if I try baseball and I'm not a natural like my dad, it doesn't mean that I'm no good at everything. I'm the best reader in my class! Even my dad says I can finish a book faster than him and that when he's not sure what a really hard word means asks me."

Now, instead of panic, there was pride in Gordon's voice.

"Exactly, but that's not to say you will definitely be bad at baseball. You haven't even tried it yet. Maybe you'll be a good player, maybe you won't. You might just have to practice harder than some of the other kids. That's not a bad thing, though. Not every rock star is born knowing how to play an instrument. It takes most people years of practice and hard work before they get really great at any one thing.

"Yea, my mom can't cook but she's a great painter. And my brother can take apart a phone and put it back together, but he's terrible at spelling."

"Right. You can't be great at every single thing in the world - unless maybe you're one of the characters in your books."

They both looked at the tall stack of paperbacks teetering on Gordon's bedside table.

A wave of exhaustion crashed over Gordon. The excitement of the past week had finally caught up with him. He rubbed his eyes under his glasses and gave a yawn fit to split his jaw.

Desmond walked up to Gordon and put his paws on his shoulder. Already mid-trance, Desmond pressed left, right, left, right. Eyes closed, purring, and listening to Gordon's slow even breathing, Desmond fell asleep.

Chapter 9

- Jeffrey's Midnight Visit -

(Spring - April 1997)

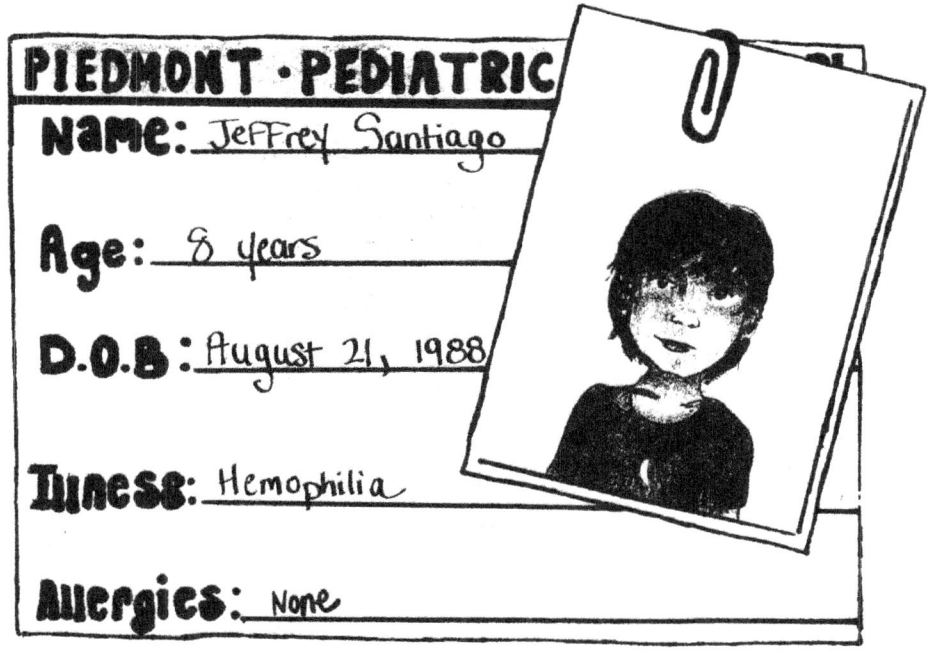

Jeffrey sat on his bed frowning. He stared at the white blankets with the pale blue checkers and crossed his arms.

"Stupid doctors," he mumbled to himself. The beeping from the machine next to him told him that the more he thought about how he had missed his class field trip, the faster his heart started to beat.

He threw himself backwards and hit his pillows with a muffled thud. Curling the ends of the pillow up over his ears, Jeffrey tried to drown out the annoying, repetitive beeping at his side. Jeffrey's eyes burned and his throat felt like he was trying to swallow a cotton ball. He thought about pressing the call button next to his bed just to force the nurse to come running for no reason.

But when Jeffrey lifted his head and reached over to repeatedly punch the nurse's button, a shadow beside his bed made him stop. The creature looked over at Jeffrey lazily before stretching its front paws up to the edge of his bed. With a swift leap, the cat jumped up onto the bed and sat at the foot of it, flicking his tail and breaking his gaze only to blink slowly and importantly.

"Dumb cat," Jeffrey said staring back at the feline. "Get on, scat!"

But the cat just licked his paw and ran it from the back of his ear to the tip of his nose a couple of times, ignoring Jeffrey's warning.

Jeffrey glared and was about to shake his legs to force the cat to move when a voice came out of the darkness.

"You know, that really is no way to greet a guest."

Jeffrey blinked at the cat who was still pawing at his ear, causing him to stop with his tongue still out and raise his silver eyes.

"Cat got your tongue?" Desmond asked smartly and his whiskers twitched as he tried not to smile.

Chapter 10
- Keeping Secrets -
(Spring - April 1997)

Desmond sat on the counter at the nurse's stand and licked the fur on his chest. He didn't bother to look up as one of the new nurses walked behind the counter and slapped down a patient's file.

"I hate cats," she said as she eyed Desmond suspiciously. "Especially *that* one."

Hearing this, Desmond took a break from his morning bath and looked at the nurse's name tag.

Brooke, he thought to himself, *I'll remember that.*

"They're so creepy," Brooke went on. "Look at him just staring at us."

Desmond now made it a point to make sure his silver eyes followed Brooke all around the nurse's station as she worked. He secretly amused himself at how clever and hilarious he was being as Brooke kept shooting nervous glances in his direction.

After nearly a half hour of annoying Brooke, Desmond got up and stretched. Teasing rude nurses was one of his specialties, but he had grown bored of it for today. Besides, Jeffrey in room 722 should have just finished breakfast, which meant that Desmond would now be allowed inside his room.

Desmond jumped down off the counter and onto the desk below. He walked across the forms Brooke was filling out and laughed to himself when she jumped up yelling about "putting this hospital's priorities back in order."

Desmond was the coolest cat on the floor. Every doctor, nurse, and custodian on the ward knew who the beautiful sleek feline was.

"Hey Des," remarked a nurse.

"G'morning, kitty cat," said a doctor.

Desmond returned the greeting by weaving through their legs as they passed.

He stopped outside of room 722 and listened. He could hear Jeffrey's mom yelling into her phone about Jeffrey's dad. She did not see Desmond walk in.

"You'd think, Alice, that he would visit his son in the hospital. I mean, he cut himself almost to the *bone*. But does he visit his son? No. Sends him a horror book, but doesn't visit. But it's not like I'm *not* going to give him a gift from his father, though, right? And *please*, let's not forget how I had to cancel my conference in Astrid Cape, Alice. *Astrid Cape*. Does he cancel his *Mars Wars* marathon? No."

Desmond could see that Jeffrey had jammed his pillow back over his head.

Well, seems as good a time as any, he thought to himself and walked further into the room.

With no effort at all, Desmond had jumped up onto Jeffrey's hospital bed. He stepped his front paws on Jeffrey's hip and began to purr and knead his side. Jeffrey lifted the pillow off of his face the tiniest bit and looked down at Desmond. Smiling, he reached out a hand and stroked the extra soft fur on his friend's chest. Desmond gave Jeffrey a slow blink, letting him know that he was here now, and would stay for as long as he was needed.

"Hang on Alice, that cat is here again. Shoo!" she yelled at Desmond, holding the phone against her shoulder with one hand and swinging at the bed with the other. Desmond just stared at her and didn't budge. Actually, he sat down.

"Atchooooo!" Jeffrey's mother sneezed. "Fine, you win. I'll leave." She grabbed her bag and hurried out of the room, yelling some more about how Jeffrey's father hadn't been to the hospital to visit him yet.

"New book, Jeff?"

Having considered it safe to remove his head from under his pillow, Jeffrey resurfaced.

"Huh?"

"Did you get a new book?" Desmond pointed at the hard cover on Jeffrey's bed tray with his eyes.

"Oh yea. My mom brought it when she came today. She said it was from my dad."

"What's this one about?"

"It's about how they used to mummify the Pharaohs in ancient Egypt. My mom says it's going to give me nightmares, but she always worries too much anyway."

"Well, she's your mom. Worrying about you is a large part of her job description."

"Mmmm," Jeffrey grunted and Desmond could tell it was time to change the subject.

"So, tell me something new."

Jeffrey sat bolt upright, a sudden gleam in his eyes. In his haste, he dislodged Desmond from the little nest he had worked in the sheets at the bend in Jeffrey's knees.

"I read that copper is sometimes used in the doorknobs of hospitals because it can kill up to 95% of your everyday germ. And did you know that some crystals have healing properties? Like jade for balance and amethyst for stress."

"Hmmm, I did not. Where'd you read that?"

"My mom brought me some books from the library about crystals, gems, minerals, stuff like that. She said I'm not likely to have bad dreams about scientists trying to grow diamonds in a laboratory."

"Well she's probably right about that. Although… she did bring you that book on the world's most dangerous insects last week, and that had some pretty nasty close-ups of creepy-crawlies." Desmond's fur shivered as he recalled a highly detailed image of fire ants consuming an animal carcass.

Jeffrey chuckled.

"It's just nature, Des. That kind of stuff doesn't bother me."

A note about Jeffrey - he *loved* facts. He loved facts about the ocean, animals, space, history, the human body, really anything that he could get his hands on. His brain was as thirsty for knowledge as the Sahara Desert was for rain (and Jeffrey would gladly tell you that the Sahara kept a regular daily temperature of about 104 degree, and a temp of about 41 degree when the sun went down).

Up until Jeffrey's first night at Piedmont Hospital, he had believed it to be a fact that cats couldn't talk. After meeting Desmond, he quickly realized that this supposed fact wasn't true in every case. Regardless of one of the world's most *seemingly* obvious facts having been proven false in Desmond's case, it did not ruin Jeffrey's appreciation of universal truths. All it did was lead Jeffrey to believe that there was much more to learn about the world around him. To him, Desmond was a cat that could talk, and give rather good advice for that matter, so that was a fact. Other cats could not talk: also a fact. This must mean that his friend Desmond was a very special feline, and that, to Jeffrey, was the most important fact of all.

It was interesting to Desmond that Jeffrey, who relied almost exclusively on proven facts, accepted with no trouble at all that Desmond's vocabulary stretched far beyond the typical "meow" of his feline brothers and sisters.

A sudden knock announced the arrival of Dotty, Desmond's favorite nurse.

"Knock knock, Jeffrey, it's 2:15. Are you ready?" Every day at quarter after two Dotty came into Jeffrey's room to check his leg and IV drip.

Jeffrey had cut his leg on a piece of glass in the playground dirt at morning recess. Since Jeffrey had a blood disease that made it hard for his body to stop bleeding when he got a cut or bruise, he had to leave school and stay at the hospital. This was so the doctors and nurses could watch him and make sure he stayed safe while they helped his body heal properly.

"Alrighty Desi, you know the drill."

This was Desmond's gentle reminder that it was time for him to go. He stood up and stretched, his rump high in the air and his front paws reaching far in front of him.

"Can't he stay, Dotty?"

"C'mon Jeff, you know I can't have him sniffing around you while I work. What if he knocks something over or bumps something already sterilized onto the ground?"

"Aww, he won't do that. He'll stay right there, at the end of my bed. Won't you Desmond?" said Jeffrey throwing a secretive smile at the cat.

"And just how do you know he'll stay? Cats are very curious creatures, downright nosy sometimes."

She does have a point, Desmond thought. But he parked his behind at Jeffrey's feet as if to say "See, Dotty? The kid's right, I promise I'll behave."

"Please, please, please? The most beautiful please with cherries and whipped cream and sugar on top?" Jeffrey pleaded. Then he said "he makes me feel safe," in a quieter voice than he had used for begging.

You could practically see Dotty's mind change instantly inside her skull.

"Fine, but the first step he takes over here will earn him a one way ticket to the other side of that door. Got it?"

"You're the best nurse in the whole world, Dotty!"

"Yea yea yea, and Ronald Grump is going to make a great president. Just don't make me regret letting him stay." Dotty said hiding a grin. She was pretending it was much more of an inconvenience for her to change her mind than it actually was - she didn't want Jeff to know how easily he had persuaded her.

"I won't, and neither will Desmond," he assured her.

Dotty smiled and gave Desmond a quick pet before washing her hands and sliding on her gloves.

Jeffrey shot a quick smirk at the cat, who blinked slowly, but with only one eye. It was his way of letting Jeffrey know that he understood and that the secret they shared was safe.

Chapter 11
- The Hockey Junkie -
(Spring - May 1997)

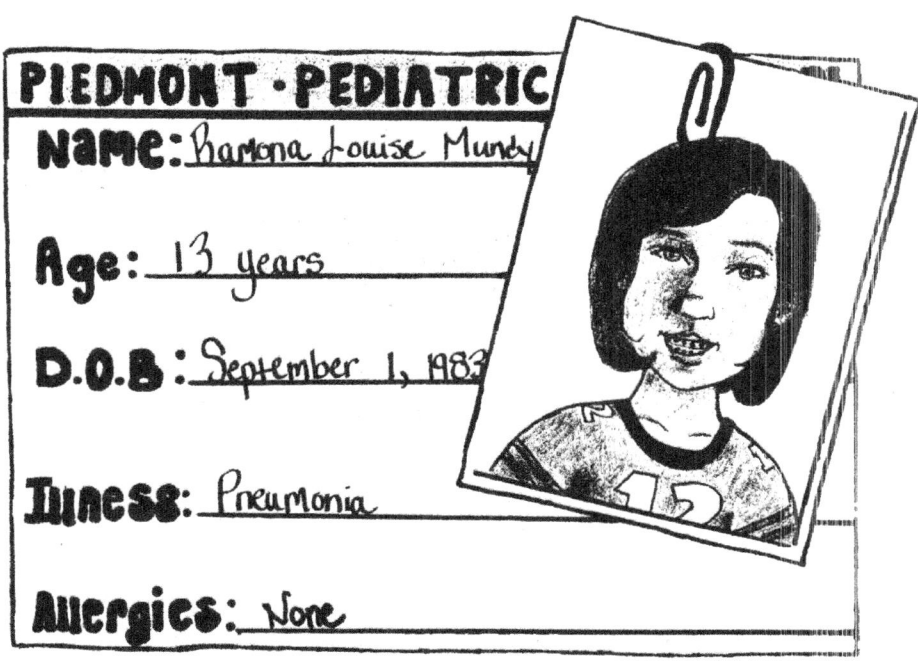

Ramona Louise Mundy was a small girl for her age, but boy was she tough. She was skinny, fast and scrappy. At 13 she was considered a hockey prodigy by her coaches.

Ramona kept her wavy hair cut short. It curled in at the ends and cupped her chin in its tips. She only wore sneakers and detested any article of clothing that made a spur-of-the-moment game of hockey unplayable. Naturally, she mostly wore her older brothers hand-me-downs.

"Desi, you're just in time! Malik is just about to score the winning shot against Stafford! One of the greatest plays in the last decade, c'mon, hurry!"

Ramona was watching old hockey games that her dad had recorded on tape for her. He had even brought in and set up an old television so she could watch them in her hospital room. Ramona was a hockey junkie, and any time not spent playing the game was time wasted. Therefore, she felt tortured by her stay on Piedmont Pediatric Ward.

She patted the bed next to her right hip and pressed 'play' with the remote.

"Look, you can see Malik over there. He's all the way at the other end of the rink doesn't even know where the puck is. Now watch. He just realized that Cambridge has it everyone laughed at him there, he almost slipped turning around - and he charges up and gets to the other side in three seconds flat! That's how he got his nickname: Jerry "The Bullet" Malik."

Desmond had close to no clue what in the world Ramona was talking about, but the excitement on her face made him pretend he understood every word. He glued his eyes to the screen and watched the players race back and forth.

"GOAL!" Ramona's arms flew up to punch the air so suddenly she knocked a bowl off the bed tray. Desmond was used to this though - Ramona cheered for every goal, even when it was scored by the opposing team. She appreciated any and every display of athletic skill, even if it meant the team she was routing for lost because of it.

Ramona paused the tape and gave her full attention to Desmond. "So, guess what?" she said.

"Tuna butt," he answered confidently.

Her laughter rang through the air like heavy church bells singing at noontime.

"No, but close. I'm actually just kidding, tuna butt is *not* close at all. Guess who the owner of a brand new, professional grade, 1997 series, Zeavenly hockey stick with non-slip-grip is?"

"I have absolutely no idea, Ramona. The anticipation is killing me... wait, could it be *you*?"

"YES! Sydney got it for me. I can't wait to try it out with her. My mom brought it by last night so I could see it. Ugh, I wish I was home so I could go outside and play."

"Soon enough. What are the doctors saying?"

"The usual," Ramona dropped her voice to mimic Dr. Clement, "'Ramona, you're a very strong girl, I'd say. In fact, you keep working as hard as you've been to get better and you'll be skating up the ice in no time!'

Ramona's voice returned to it's normal pitch. "But he doesn't actually say *when* I'll get outta here."

"Makes sense. He probably doesn't want to get your hopes up by telling you a specific date in case it changes," reasoned Desmond.

"Yea, but Sydney's family is going on vacation in only a week and they said if I'm better by then, I can go. They're gonna go to the *History of Hockey Hotspot*. I've wanted to go there since my first time on the ice!"

She fell back onto her pillows, her fingers laced behind her head.

"I really hope I get out of here soon, Des." Desmond could tell that Ramona was headed towards sulk city if the subject didn't change soon.

"What, you don't like hanging out with me?" The cat's attempt at humor sort of worked; he noticed a smile flicker across Ramona's face.

"Nah, Des. It's not that. You're the only thing that makes this place half bearable. I would've gone crazy by now if it weren't for you." A good hard chin scratch for Desmond confirmed that Ramona meant what she said.

"Put the game back on. I wanna see Stepford's face again when he realizes Morton scored right between his knees."

Ramona rolled her eyes but laughed, "It's Stafford and Malik, Des, not Stepford and Morton."

"You know what I mean."

Desmond settled himself on Ramona's lap and got comfortable. If he knew Ramona even a little - and he thought he knew her pretty well - they would probably watch at least two more games after this one.

And they did.

Chapter 12

- All's Fair in Love and Hockey -

(Spring - June 1997)

"It's not FAIR!"

WHAM! A plastic cup flew out of room 710 and exploded against the opposite wall.

"It's just - it's just not *fair*! How could she do that? I - hate - her!"

The last sentence was punctured by heavy sobs - Desmond picked up his pace. As he entered the room, a plump nurse came bustling out. She was muttering wildly under her breath.

"So much for 'don't shoot the messenger.' You'd think I wrote that letter to her, but no! I only *delivered* it!"

Looking past the nurse a sad scene greeted Desmond's light eyes. Ramona was curled up on her side hugging her pillow. Her eyes were streaming and blotchy, and tremendous gasps ripped through her body as if it were made of paper and glass instead of skin and bone.

Desmond thought she must be terribly sick and that something was horribly wrong. Then he remembered what he heard the nurse saying as she left and he realized that Ramona was only crying.

Without saying a word Desmond leapt onto her bed and pushed his head into hers. She was crying so loud it hurt Desmond's ears to be that close, but he imagined how bad Ramona must feel inside, so he didn't stop.

Eventually, Ramona calmed down.

"I - hate - her - Des," she croaked out thickly.

"Who?"

"Sydney," Ramona practically spat the word.

"Why? She's your best friend," he reasoned.

"*Was* my best friend." She unfolded a crumpled piece of paper to set in front of th cat, because of course he could read as well as he spoke.

Here's what he read:

Dear Ramona,

        I hope you're feeling okay. I'm really bummed that you can't come with us o vacation. My parents said that if the History of Hockey Hotspot is as cool as they say, they migh take us back in a couple of years so you can see it too! Since you're not able to go, my parents tol me I could bring someone else from the team. I asked Kara if she wanted to come. She said she' been there before twice (she has an aunt who lives near there that her family goes to visit) but tha she'd NEVER say no to a trip to the Hotspot. I waited until the absolute last minute to ask her i case the doctors let you come home. Believe me, I'd much rather have you come than Kara and I'n really sad that we won't get to see it for the first time together. Anyway, I'll send you a postcard an take lots of pictures to show you when I get back.

    Love,

    Your very best friend in the whole wide world, Sydney

        XOXOXOXOX

"Oh no," Desmond said when he had finished. "I know how bad you wanted to go."

He pawed the letter to the floor, curled up against Ramona's chest, and snuggled his head under her chin.

"It's not even that, really. Well, I don't know. I - she shouldn't have invited stupid old Kara. She was wrong to do that."

"Why's that wrong?"

"Because, *I* was supposed to be the one going with her."

"But you can't go Ramona. I'm sorry to say that, but the doctors want to keep you a couple more days to see how the new antibiotics work."

"I know, but - " she shook with anger.

"But… what?"

Her delicate face twisted in thought. It was like she was trying to figure out how to say something, or maybe how to not say anything at all.

"But we were supposed to go *together*. It would have been *both* our first times there and we would have gotten to see it all with *each other*. But now she went and invited Kara and she's been there *twice* already! She's probably going to boss Sydney around to all the things she wants to do since she knows the place."

Hot tears rolled down Ramona's pink cheeks. Every couple of inhales, a breath would hiccup in her throat.

"It's okay to be upset about it, Ramona."

"I just - I thought she was my best friend, but best friends don't betray each other."

"Do you really think her inviting Kara was a betrayal? And even if you do, do you think she did it to hurt you?"

"Yes."

"Think about it, Ramona. Pretend you were her for a minute: her best friend - thats right, I said it - her *best* friend, meaning you, has been sick in the hospital for almost two weeks. She's probably very lonely and bored without you. Even though she hates that you can't go with her, she still wants to be able to share the experience with someone. I can't imagine that she'd go out of her way to make you upset. In fact, she'd probably be incredibly upset herself if she knew how you were feeling right now."

"Well that's the thing, Des. She doesn't know how I'm feeling because she didn't think about it *or* me when she invited Kara. If I have to put myself in her shoes, why didn't she put herself in mine? Why didn't she realize how hurtful she was being. I would've known I'd be hurt if I was her."

"You're two different people, Ramona. You won't always think or feel the same way about everything. Something might upset her that you don't think is a big deal and vise versa."

"Hmph," Ramona was running out of steam. Desmond didn't think she really wanted to stay mad at Sydney, but she was hurting so bad.

"You don't have to forgive her today, or stop feeling hurt or mad - you're entitled to your feelings. I just wouldn't give up on your friendship completely. Not yet, at least."

Four days later Ramona got another letter in the mail. This time, Desmond was there when the nurse handed it to her. She didn't wait for her to open it before speed walking to the door and shutting it behind her.

The envelope read "RAMONA MUNDY."

"It's from Sydney."

When she opened the envelope a postcard and three pictures fell out. Each one snapped an image of a girl with very long, straight black hair. In one picture the girl was standing next to a large hockey player who was missing several teeth. She was holding up a picture of Ramona to make it seem as if she were there too. In the other picture, the girl was eating French fries and a hotdog off a giant hockey puck posing as a plate. Included in that picture was the portrait of Ramona propped against a glass behind her own hockey puck plate with matching hotdog and fries. The last picture showed Sydney in a hockey uniform that was much too big for her. The helmet was so big for her head it had slid down over her eyes. All you could see of her face was her smile. Sure enough, the picture of Ramona had been placed in a helmet and set on the bench next to Sydney. The rest of the uniform was laid out underneath.

Ramona grabbed the first picture.

"This is 'The Bullet!' How'd she get a picture with him? Oh my gosh, that's so lucky! But look - she's holding my picture up like *I'm* there!"

She picked up the second photo.

"And here we are at *Lucky Puck Pub*," she held up the picture of her and Sydney behind their hotdogs.

"And that's us in the Flying Foxes' team uniforms from when they won the Stanby Cup in 1960. I'm wearing jersey #30 - that's Evan Liliky! Sydney's wearing numero uno, #1. That's Dorian Griffith."

"It amazes me how much you know about this game," Desmond said in quiet admiration. Ramona didn't even hear him.

"That's so cool that she did that! I wonder where Kara is. She's not in any of these."

"If you ask me, I'd say that Sydney's been putting herself in your shoes," said Desmond wisely.

"What do you mean?"

"Think about it. How would you feel if when you opened that letter, you saw a bunch of pictures of Sydney and Kara?"

"I think I'd feel awful, like I'd wanna curl up and shrivel away to nothin'."

"Exactly, Ramona. I think she thought about that and made sure to send you pictures that showed how much she misses you. Looks to me like she really wishes you were there."

"Yea…. it does look like that," Ramona admitted while trying not to smile *too* much at the pictures.

Chapter 13

- A Boom, a Tap and a Talking Cat -

(Spring - May 1997)

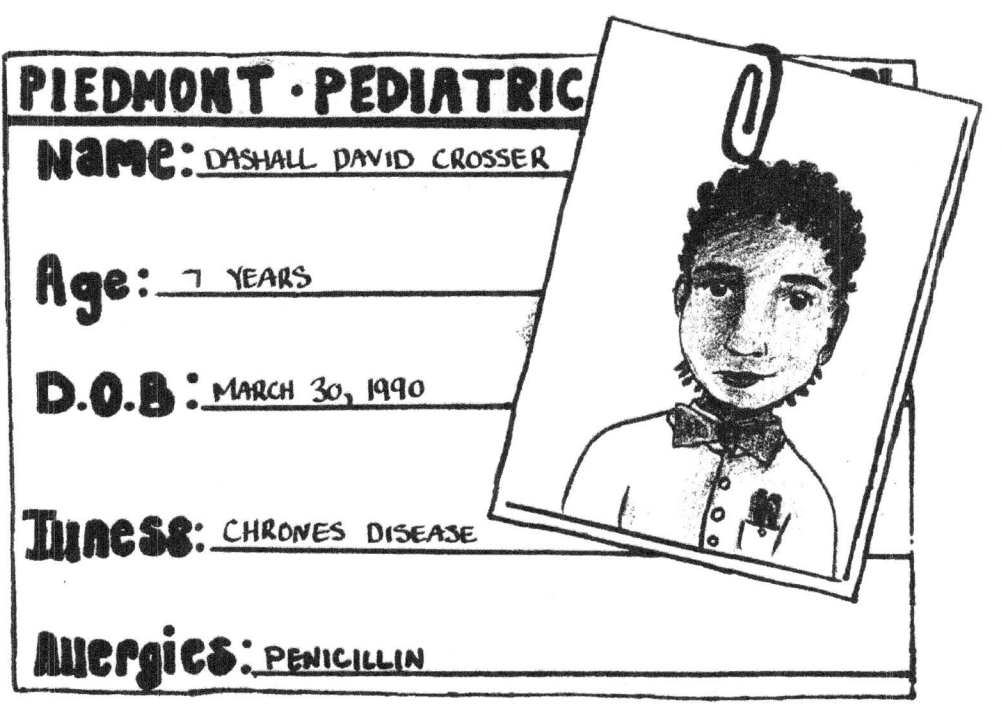

"Dashall David Crosser, please stop that racket."

"I can't mama, I need to practice."

"Mama needs a break, sweet pea."

"Okay," Dashall put down the pencils he had been using as drum sticks. The room was quiet, quiet enough that Dashall's mom closed her eyes. Dashall didn't want to rest though, so he looked around the room instead.

This is so boring, he thought.

Then, *I wish I had a snack, like ice cream or cookies.*

Finally, Dashall wondered, *how does the song for that new cookie commercial go?*

Was it *Beat Beat Bam Tap Tap*?

Or maybe *Beat Ta-Tap Tap Boom Boom?*

"Dash..."

"Sorry, mama," Dashall didn't realize he had started drumming his bed tray with his hands.

"It's alright," his mom said, pulling her body out of the chair with great effort. "I've got to pick your sister up from karate anyway. You'll be okay until Daddy comes after work? You know which button to press if you need the nurse, right?"

"Yea, I'll be good," said Dashall. Mrs. Crosser kissed her son's forehead and walked towards the door.

"Oh! Hey there, Desmond. You keep an eye on my Dash now, ya' hear?" Desmond locked eyes with the woman for only a couple of seconds before blinking and then proceeding into the room - this was Desmond's way of saying "roger that."

"Hey Desmond! Listen to this!" Dashall picked up the pencils he had been using earlier and began beating the bedside tray, the railing, an empty glass that sat on the table and even the machine beeping out his heartbeat.

Clink Boom Tap Tap

Clink Boom Tap Tap

Clink de-Boom de-Boom de-Boom Tap Tap
Thunk!

Dashall looked up at Desmond, his brilliant smile flashing as he waited for the cat's approval.

"Wow, Dash, I'm impressed. You're getting so much better," he remarked.

"I do have lots of time to practice," Dashall reminded him.

"Oh, I know. I can hear you all the way down the hall sometimes."

Dashall suddenly felt a bit embarrassed, but Desmond went on.

"I like it, though. Get's too quiet on this floor sometimes. It's nice, trust me."

"My hands just don't like sitting still. They always wanna move!"

"I'm sure. You've got so much music in you, it's got to work it's way out somehow."

"Exactly, or else I'd just explode!" Dashall slapped both hands to his cheeks and dropped his jaw.

"Don't do that. Don't explode, it'd be much too messy."

Dashall laughed. "I won't, I was just kidding."

"Well that's a relief," Desmond smiled back. He appreciated that as young as Dashall was, the boy enjoyed his dry humor.

"So what's new, Des? Catch any mice?"

"Nah, this hospital hasn't had a rodent problem since 1983. Says so on a sign out by the nurses' station. So, no, no mice. But a big fat cricket did hop out of the elevator this morning. That was fun to chase around, much more exciting than old surgical masks and plastic gloves."

"Is that cause gloves and masks don't move?"

"Oh, absolutely. In the wild I'd be a gloriously skilled hunter, a feared predator. A cat can't get much satisfaction from pouncing on a crumpled piece of rubber. It'd be like playing the drums but not hearing the beats. Something would be missing."

"Don't you get bored then?"

"Yes, sometimes, but when I do, I come visit you, or Jeffrey, or Ramona. There's lots of people to visit even if there aren't many mice to hunt and catch."

"My mama hates mice."

"Most humans do. I figure that's why they put a sign out there for everyone to see. Showing off that they've been 'Vermin Free since '83' must make people want to come here instead of going to another hospital that has rats in the halls. You know, some people even get mad that *I'm* here."

"But you're not a rat or a mouse even - you're a cat!"

"Yes, but not everyone likes animals, and *some* people definitely don't like cats. There was this woman once, I'd never met her a day in my life, and she hated me as soon as she saw me. Thought I was trying to attack a little girl. Called me a wild animal and everything."

"Why? What did you do?"

"Well, I had a friend here, like how I'm friends with you, and she got very sick and I didn't want to leave her. They made me, and I wasn't happy about it and I growled at Dr. Clement."

Dashall stared wide-eyed in disbelief. "I've never heard you growl before."

"Probably because I've never been so scared before as I was that day."

"What made you so scared to leave? You don't seem scared when the nurses make you leave my room."

"I guess it was because that day I had a bad feeling. I had a bad feeling that my friend wasn't going to be okay."

"Was she?... Okay, I mean?" Dashall whispered even though he seemed to already know the answer.

"No, she died." Desmond's breath caught in his throat. He had never told anyone about this before.

"I didn't get to say goodbye," he added. Desmond wasn't sure why he felt he needed to say that.

And then something wonderful happened. Dashall opened his arms wide, welcoming Desmond into them. Desmond had always been the one to comfort the kids, but here was a boy offering comfort to Desmond, who accepted.

The cat crawled into Dashall's lap and felt two tiny arms wrap around and hug him to his chest. Desmond could feel Dashall's heart beating strong in his chest.

Ba-bum Ba-bum Ba-bum Ba-bum

He could feel a soft purr bubbling up from deep inside his own body.

Dashall kept hugging Desmond until his purring was so loud that a nurse passing by the open door could hear it spilling out from inside. Dashall could feel it vibrating in his bones.

It kept a slow steady rhythm that made Dashall's hands itch to start patting out a beat. But his hands were too busy hugging, so he tapped his feet instead.

Chapter 14

- A Feline's Fragile Feelings -

(Spring - May 1997)

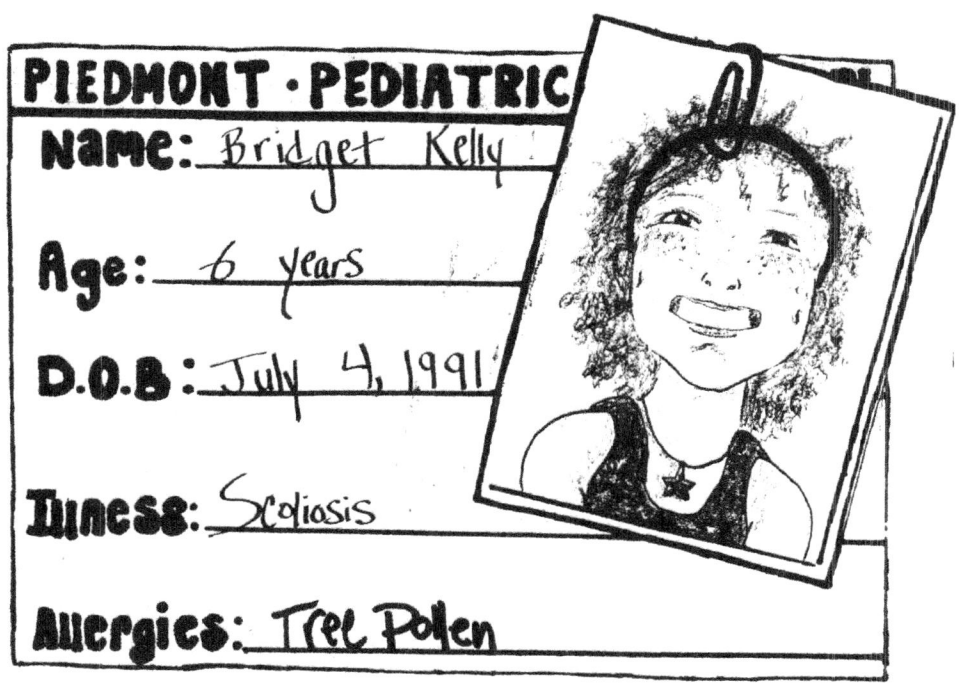

Desmond the cat slunk around the nurse's station, his head low. The moonlight was almost as silvery-blue as his fur.

Scratch Scratch and a low *hisssss*.

Desmond bent his legs and crept towards the door, making no sound whatsoever. He was in predator mode.

I've got you now, he thought as he ran silently across the room and paused at the side of the bed.

Scratch scratch, came the noise again. The cat lowered his shoulders and pinpointed the exact location of the noise above.

Crouch, thought Desmond. *Get feet in ready position, and.... JUMP!*

Desmond's paws clasped around a tiny hand.

"Desmond!"

The cat lifted his paws and sighed when he saw the skinny fingers underneath.

"Bridget," Desmond said as he sat up and twitched his tail, "remember what we talked about?"

"Yes," the little girl sighed as she leaned on her elbow and reached a hand toward the cat. "Say your name when I call you so that you know it's just me and not a mouse," she recited tonelessly and dropped her arm.

"Exactly. You don't want to go hurting a cat's pride you know. We are very skilled hunters and your fingers rustling around on your bed sheets pretending to be a mouse could be insulting to some felines. We *are* a rather dignified breed."

"Sorry Desi," Bridget whispered and extended her fingers again.

"That being said," Desmond said as he began to walk over to her, "it's nothing a good chin scratch can't fix."

Bridget scratched behind Desmond's ears and under his chin. She petted him from the top of his head to the tip of his tail. In no time at all, Desmond's purr filled the room. He laid on Bridget's shoulder and nestled his head under her chin.

After a while, Bridget spoke.

"My surgery's tomorrow, Des."

Desmond made sure that his purring did not falter. He rubbed his cheek against her jaw and fanned out his fingers, pressing them into her shoulder.

"I'll be there after, when you wake up, Bridget. I won't leave until you're ready - or until the doctors kick me out."

Bridget snuggled under her blankets before she reached her hand up to Desmond's face and pressed her thumb in the divot between his eyes, massaging up and down. He leaned into her touch and closed his eyes.

"Promise you'll stay here 'til I go down to surgery tomorrow?" She asked, her eyes already closed and sleep creeping into her voice.

"I promise," and with that, Desmond gave one last yawn and curled his tail up over his eyes.

Chapter 15

- Shades of Melrose -

(Summer - July 1997)

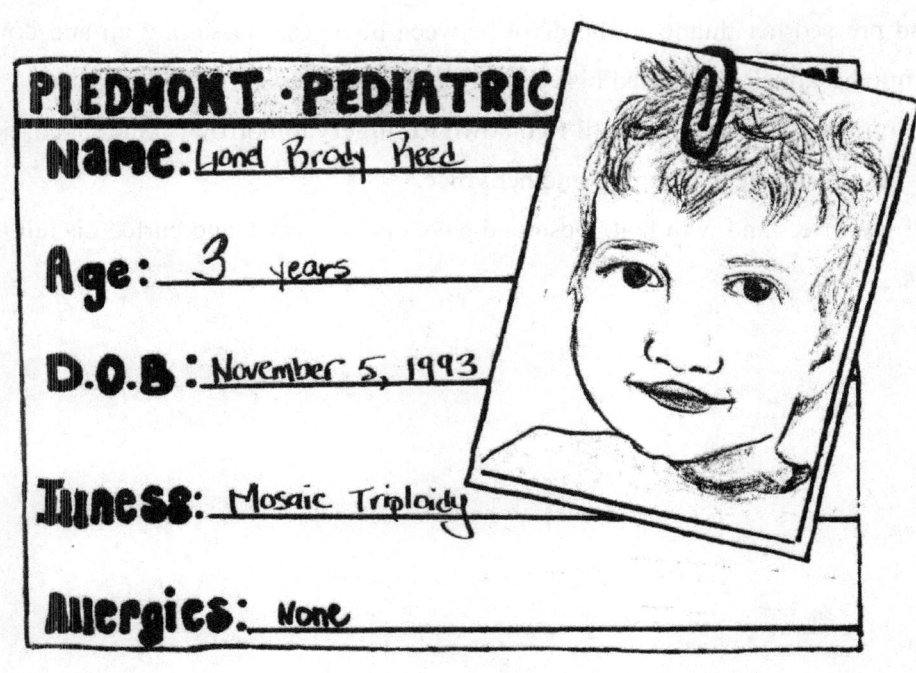

Lionel Reed was a model patient. He delighted everyone he encountered at Piedmont Hospital during his stays. He woke up from surgery smiling and had courage that could rival a lion.

"Lionel…. such a fitting name," the nurses would say.

"What a brave name for brave boy," they'd gush.

Lionel was not *just* a model patient. He was a remarkably wonderful child. At three years old, he did not speak and he did not walk. He was about half the size of a boy his age, but he could put a smile on the grumpiest of faces. It was through this, his rare ability to spread happiness with just a grin, that Lionel reminded Desmond of Melrose.

Since Lionel didn't talk, Desmond did all of the talking when they were together. The cat would dazzle Lionel by re-telling the stories that Gordon had once read out loud. When whispering the tales into his ear, Lionel would laugh such a hearty laugh, his mother might turn around and look curiously at the baby before chuckling herself.

Lionel's mother and father adored Desmond. They relished the time he would spend in Lionel's room and would often invite him onto their own laps for a good pet.

For his part, Desmond had never loved any of the parents he'd met more than Mr. and Mrs. Reed. He had also never seen any parents as devoted and hopelessly in love with their son like this couple. Parents who offer such unconditional love and delight for their child are hard to come by, and Desmond had a feeling that was why Lionel was the way he was. He had only ever known love and support, so how could he give out anything else?

When Lionel was born, he'd been too early and too tiny. He'd been born with a disease called Mosaic Triploidy, something doctors didn't figure out until later. It wasn't their fault though- it was an extremely rare illness and only several dozen cases were ever reported in the world. Desmond was pretty sure it had to do with chromosomes, and maybe having too many of them. Whatever the illness was exactly, it didn't stop Lionel from being the happiest, friendliest kid around.

On Lionel's 6th visit since he'd met the talking cat, Desmond was laying with the top half of his body on the toddler's chest.

This kid sleeps like a log, he thought and he yawned loudly.

Mr. Reed was sleeping behind his newspaper when Mrs. Reed walked in.

"Arthur," she said softly.

Mr. Reed snorted and woke with a start. "Wha-what? Oh, uh, I've been awake the whole time," he said with confidence.

Mrs. Reed swatted his excuse away as if she were swatting a fly out of the air.

"Oh, never mind, lazy bones. I don't care if you were sleeping. Has the doctor been in?"

"Nope, not yet," Mr. Reed rubbed his eyes.

"Good, I want to ask him something when he comes back." She pushed the blonde hair from her sleeping son's forehead. Then her hand moved to Desmond, who leaned in for a thorough scratching.

"There's a new patient in 702, Arty." Desmond's eyes stayed closed but his ears perked up. "Little girl. I think her name's Olive, but don't hold me to that - I did have a Greek salad for lunch."

Mr. Reed chuckled, "I won't Emily. Do you know why she's here? Do I *want* to know why she's here?"

"Do you ever?"

"Good point."

"She's here to see if she's a candidate for a tumor removal surgery. She's only nine Arthur.

Mr. Reed let out a sigh so big it was like he'd been holding it in for days. His lips made a straight line and he looked at the floor.

"I hate being a part of this world, constantly having to be reminded of how unfair life can be. Seeing this kind of stuff happen to kids."

Desmond made a mental note to visit room 702 later that night, when visiting hours were over and the night nurse was reading her romance novel.

Until then, he was going to sit on Mr. Reed's lap and swat at the corners of his newspaper. The man always got a kick out of that.

Chapter 16
- The Cold Shoulder -
(Summer - July 1997)

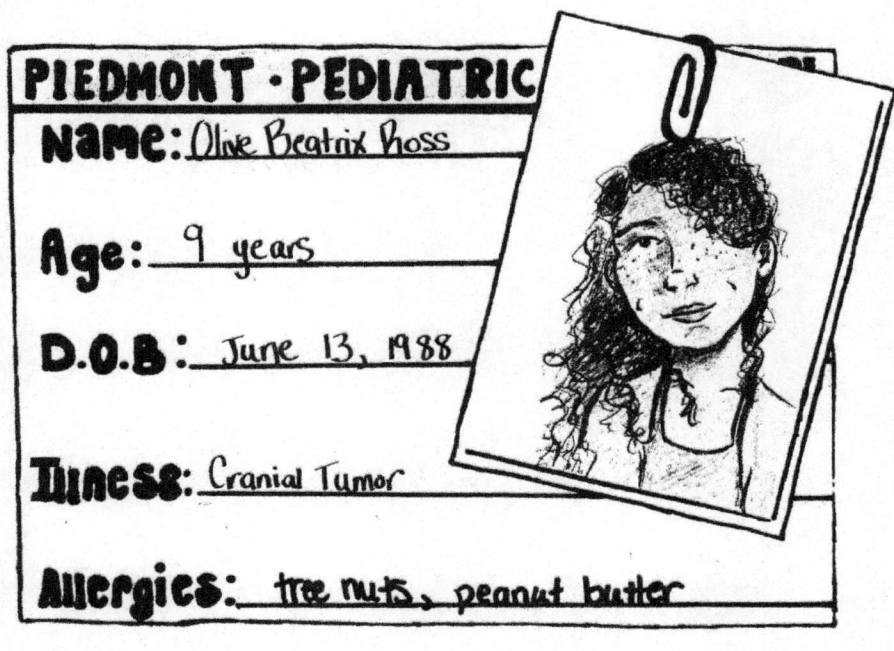

Desmond slunk through the hallways like a ghost. He'd overheard that Brooke was working overnight to cover a shift for Denise, and Desmond wouldn't mind giving her a healthy scare, especially after the dirty look she gave him when she saw him washing his tail earlier.

It's just nature, Brooke he thought to himself and was reminded at once of Jeffrey.

Lucky, thought Desmond as he scampered into room 702 - he hadn't passed Brooke on his way.

"Meow," he said to announce his presence. The girl stirred.

"Meow," he said again once he was on the bed at her feet.

"Not now, kitty," she said.

"If not now, then when?" Desmond asked, thinking himself rather clever.

No response.

He cleared his throat: "I heard tell your name was Olive. I enjoy the green ones, and 'm Desmond."

Again, no response.

Even if I wasn't a talking cat, thought Desmond, *it's very rude to ignore someone like this.*

"Salmon is pink,

Wee mice are brown,

Between cats and dogs,

Felines take the crown!"

All was quiet. The girl didn't even move.

That took me three days to think up, thought Desmond.

"Please kitty, I need to sleep. 'Mm so tired."

Fine thought Desmond, not bothering to say it out loud. He left, his feline pride wounded and his feelings hurt.

Chapter 17
- The Disconnect -
(Summer - July 1997)

"Yep, right in the middle of her brain. Smack dab in the amygdala."

Desmond wished the doctors would find another place to discuss their patients.

"Olive yea, Olive Ross. Goes by Ollie. Came in the other day. Her parents were clos to hysterics saying that we were the last place that could help her."

Olive? That girl who ignored me the other night?

Desmond hadn't been back since then - he was pretty embarrassed and was nursing a wounded ego - every kid he'd met so far had thought it was pretty cool to befriend a talking cat.

But what was it that Dr. Clement just said about her amygdala? The amygdala wa the part of the brain responsible for a human's emotional response, among other things Desmond knew that because for 3 months last year, he listened to an intern recite medica facts under his breath.

Maybe she can't hear you, suggested a voice in Desmond's head.

If Olive had a tumor in her brain, maybe that stopped her from being able t understand him. Maybe she wasn't ignoring him at all.

This gave Desmond an idea. He didn't care that it was daytime; he walked right int Olive's room and announced "Olive, if you can hear me, you are listening to a talking cat and you have gone totally and completely bonkers. The only thing that can save you is to clap 3 times. Quick! You only have 5 more seconds!"

Olive sat up and looked at Desmond.

"Here, kitty kitty, pst pst pst." She rubbed her fingers together to get him to jump up. It seemed like she had heard him, but she wasn't clapping to save herself from madness. Desmond jumped onto the table by her bed and then onto the mattress. He decided to be blunt.

"Can you hear me, Olive? Do you know what I'm saying?"

"Oh, don't be mad, kitty. I'm sorry for the other night. I didn't mean to shoo you away. I've been hoping you'd come back ever since. Will you forgive me?"

She snuggled her face into Desmond's neck. Her long honey brown hair tickled Desmond's whiskers when she hugged him.

They were definitely having two different conversations.

"C'mon kitty, I'm sorry."

Desmond accepted then that Ollie couldn't hear him. The doctors didn't say anything about Ollie's ears not working, just about the tumor inside her head. Then again, Desmond didn't really know what made kids able to hear him. When he was young, he had thought that Mel's ears were special, the only ones that could understand him, but after meeting Gordon he had to consider that it was something else entirely.

So Olive couldn't hear him. Big deal. She seemed perfectly happy to run her hands through his fur and bury her face in the silky hair on his neck.

Naturally, with Desmond being a cat, and an extremely sensitive one at that, he began to purr and the two spent the rest of the afternoon together.

Chapter 18
- Honeybees and Lemon Meringue Pie -
(Summer - July 1997)

Over the next couple of days, Desmond spent most of his time in Olive's room. Their relationship was the complete opposite of his and Lionel's. Since Olive couldn't understand the talking cat, *she* did all the talking. She told him all about her mom and her dad, her twin cousins who lived around the block from her, and her pet hamster, Uma.

"You'd probably love Uma, Desmond. Well… you'd probably love chasing her around."

Desmond silently agreed. From the sound of Ollie's stories, hamsters were not much different from mice.

The first time Desmond met Ollie's parents he was pleased to find them very kind and interesting people. They couldn't stay for long because they both had to get back to work, but he very much enjoyed the time spent in their company.

Ollie's dad, Mr. Ross was very tall and thin. He had light wispy hair and a surprisingly full beard. He was a biology professor at a highly respectable university, and when he wasn't teaching, he spent most of his time studying bees. He would often remind Ollie that "our planet couldn't keep going without them, my little honey bee."

Ollie's mother, on the other hand, was the head chef for an elegant restaurant called "Sit Down and Eat." She worked too many hours too many days a week, or that's what

Ollie said at least. Mrs. Ross had dark skin soft as velvet and her eyes were the color of coffee with just a splash of creamer.

Ollie sat smack in the middle of the pair, a quiet combination of her parents. Her hair hung in loose curls that spiraled toward the ends and was darker than her father's, but not so curly as her mother's. It was like sunlight streaming through molten caramel. She was a remarkable girl, but, unfortunately, she had a remarkably stubborn tumor.

"You tried chemo and radiation, huh? The whole thing?" Dr. Clement confirmed with Ollie's parents the next time they were both at the hospital.

"Yes, for almost two years, starting when she was 4. It just got worse and she was horribly sick the *whole* time. We couldn't keep putting her through that, so we stopped and have been trying to find a doctor to just remove the darn thing, but no one is willing to go near it!" said Mrs. Ross, for what felt to her like the 100th time.

"Well, I can see why it's taken you so long to find a doctor willing to take it out. Its carved out a home in a particularly tricky spot."

"But you're willing to try," Mrs. Ross said and it was not a question.

Dr. Clement twirled his mustache like he usually did when he was thinking hard about something.

"Yes, I'll try," he said at last.

Mr. and Mrs. Ross hugged. They both looked ready to cry - Mrs. Ross' eyes were reaching a tipping point.

"Thank you, *so so* much," Mr. Ross shook Dr. Clement's hand clumsily.

"Now hold on, I'm not saying it'll definitely work. I might start and find there's no way to proceed without… well… killing her. And even if I do manage to get the whole thing out, it's possible she won't wake up afterwards."

"We know. We've had a dozen doctors tell us those exact things, but you're the only doctor who's willing to try," explained Mrs. Ross.

"You've given us some hope again, Doc."

Dr. Clement shuffled his feet. The room felt suddenly very hot to him. He secretly second guessed his decision to try to perform the surgery. There was such a small chance it would work and the way the Ross' were looking at him it was as if he had already finished the surgery and saved their daughter! But Dr. Clement wouldn't give up now.

"We can perform the surgery this Friday. There's no point in waiting any longer. Let's not give it any more time to grow."

"My thoughts exactly," agreed Mr. Ross, then "Lucille, I'm going to have to take off the rest of the week. My research partner will be angry enough to curse me - we've started some new studies on the 'waggle dance' and he'll gripe about having to cover my classes."

"I know what you mean," said Mrs. Ross. "We have a huge event that we're catering for the mayor. They want 225 slices of our famous lemon merengue pie and the new hire can barely peel a potato let alone prepare our famous dessert. But oh well. They'll just have to suck it up. Cry me a river, build me a bridge, and get over it. My baby needs me."

"Mmmm lemon meringue pie," rumbled Dr. Clement. "My wife, Dr. Weston and I she works on this floor as well - we had the most delicious lemon meringue pie at our wedding last spring. It was to die for."

"Well, I'll just have to bring you a piece of ours and you can decide which one you like better," offered Mrs. Ross.

"It'll knock your socks off," Mr. Ross assured him. "It's her family's secret recipe passed down three generations. *I* don't even know what's in it, but it's heaven on a plate so I don't ask any questions, s'long as she keeps making it."

"I'll have to take you up on that, Lucille. I'd never say no to dessert, especially when it brings back such happy memories of last June."

"I'd be happy to bring in a slice for you," smiled Mrs. Ross.

Mr. Ross clapped his hands together. "Sounds like a plan. I better taste it too though Lulu, you know - just to make sure it's good enough to give to Dr. Clement... so he can get a good comparison."

"Gregory Ross, I bring you home lemon meringue pie from work at least four times a week."

"And it's good every time. Well! Thanks again Doc, we'll *beeee* here bright and early on Friday," said Mr. Ross, amused at his own joke.

Chapter 19
- Moonlit Hikes -
(Summer - July 1997)

It was the night before Ollie's surgery. The silence that hushed the 7th floor was deafening. It squeezed the breath out of the hospital like a cruel snake.

Desmond had spent all day sitting with Ollie. She didn't talk much and Desmond knew it was because she was scared. Ollie got quiet sometimes - she would go off into her own head and think to herself.

Around 11:00pm Desmond fell asleep. He'd thought that Ollie had fallen asleep too because her breath had been coming slow and steady for a good bit and she hadn't stirred in a while.

Ollie was in fact *not* sleeping, but deep in thought and just staring at the ceiling. Desmond didn't realize this until he woke up just over two hours later.

"I can't sleep, Kitty," she whispered.

Desmond hated that he couldn't talk to Ollie. She needed him. How was he supposed to help her if she couldn't hear him? He could only flick his tail and hope she would know he was listening.

"Even if I could sleep I wouldn't wanna. I might fall asleep tomorrow and never wake up. So I don't wanna waste tonight sleeping if that's gonna be the case."

Ollie was quiet. Desmond flicked his tail again.

"I watched a movie once when I was little about this man who always wanted to go on these adventures. His friends could never keep up with him and they would get so mad, cause he would never wanna stop to rest. 'We don't wanna go! We wanna sleep!' - that's what one of his friends said when he tried to get them to go on a moonlit hike after they'd spent the day rock-climbing. And the guy said 'I'll sleep when I'm dead!' and went hiking without them. It plays in my head like a broken record, what he said - 'I'll sleep when I'm dead… I'll sleep when I'm dead.' I don't wanna sleep yet, Des. I've never been on a moonlit hike."

The entire time Ollie had been talking she'd been concentrating on scratching the silky scruff under Desmond's chin. His heart ached to be able to talk to her, to try to provide some words of comfort.

Instead, he walked up to her face and rubbed his cheek against hers. He purred thickly and pressed his head into her neck, laying against her shoulder. She leaned into him and buried her face in his fur. She stopped talking then, but she didn't go to sleep and neither did Desmond - he flicked his tail gently on her wrist so she'd know he'd stay awake as long as she needed.

Chapter 20
- Close Only Counts in Horseshoes -
(Summer - July 1997)

She must be awake by now, Desmond thought as he scurried down the hallway.

Yes, he thought triumphantly as he saw Dr. Clement turning into room 702. A few moments later and Desmond had arrived as well.

Ollie was laying on the bed. She had bandages wrapped around her head and her eyes were closed. Tubes ran into her nose to help her breathe. Mr. Ross had his arm around Mrs. Ross. He was looking at the floor and Mrs. Ross had her hands over her face.

"While we knew this was a possibility, I honestly cannot express how sorry I am. There is a chance she could wake up. It's not very good, but then again, there wasn't a very good chance we would ever be able to remove the whole thing."

After an awkward pause, Dr. Clement continued.

"Uh, well…. alright. We'll just give you some time then. Please let us know if you need anything. Nurses will be in regularly to monitor her progress."

Two nurses and the doctor filed out of the room. Desmond didn't notice he was following them until Dr. Clement went to shut the door. He caught a last look at the silent trio before the door clicked shut. He too felt that the Ross' should be alone right now.

Chapter 21
- The Cricket Catastrophe -
(Summer - July 1997)

Desmond waited by the elevator door. He had made a game for himself by leaping up and pressing the elevator buttons that lined the wall. He would send it down to the basement, where it was cold and damp and where some of the employees of the hospital parked, and then jab the 'up' button to bring the giant metal box back to the 7th floor. He played this repetitive game because every so often it would carry up a cricket that had jumped in many floors below.

Desmond would run in and pounce before the bug ever suspected the cat lurking just beyond the doors. It was great fun whenever the doors opened to reveal a big crunchy insect, but as it was a pretty rare occurrence, most of the game was spent jumping at the buttons over and again. But it was a great distraction for times when Desmond was feeling stressed or sad, or even just plain old bored.

Desmond was just about to give up for the night when *Ding!* the doors rolled open.

Not one, but two fat crickets sat inside. Desmond lowered his shoulders, raised his rump, and pounced - but he missed. The other cricket flickered in the corner of his vision and he turned, jumping spastically into the air. This was more stimulation than Desmond was used to and in his confusion he jumped up and accidentally hit the 'down' button on the inside of the elevator!

Before he even knew what was happening the doors had closed and the meta[l] machine began rumbling its way toward the basement. Desmond froze, his every sens[e] alert and waiting.

Finally, the doors opened onto a strange scene. A forest of those metal rectangles h[e] always saw on the roads below when looking out the hospital windows stared back at him. These ones weren't moving though. They were still and dark and cast long black shadow[s] across the ground.

But, as you know, Desmond was a very curious cat. He was also very smart an[d] realized he could easily work the elevator to get himself back up to the 7th floor wheneve[r] he was ready.

For now, he wanted to explore, so explore he did.

Desmond left the light of the elevator behind and entered the musty chill of th[e] parked cars. What Desmond found was one of the greatest surprises of his life: dozens o[f] crickets hopped around on the concrete floor among the maze of painted metal.

Desmond was in heaven. He chased, pounced, bounced and leapt for nearly a hal[f] hour before a scratchy rumble broke the silence. A cough and sputter echoed against th[e] walls and the rumble got louder and deeper. Lights flashed on and Desmond was froze[n] like ice.

When the lights rounded on him, Desmond's heart flew wildly against his ribs[,] battering the bones that caged it inside. The two pale yellow lights stared him down like [a] set of merciless eyes. He knew he needed to move but he just couldn't!

Run! his brain screamed at his feet, but they didn't seem to hear it.

The lights were coming so fast they would soon be on top of Desmond. His leg[s] must've finally received the message his brain had been shouting because they propelle[d] him forward. The last couple inches of his tail brushed the front tire.

Desmond didn't stop running once he was out of the way, but sprinted to the elevato[r,] punched the 'up' button and willed his heart to slow down before it burst.

The doors opened not a moment too soon to deposit Desmond onto Piedmont Pediatric Ward. He ran out of the elevator vowing never to leave the 7th floor again. Crickets were not worth *that*.

Now it was his stomach's turn to start hollering at him.

Hmm, I missed supper, he realized, feeling starved.

Walking past a large glass window that stretched all the way from the floor to the ceiling, Desmond took a moment to admire himself, as cats sometimes liked to do.

"Hello Handsome," he said to his reflection as he modeled past. Something was off, however. He sat very close to the window and studied the silver cat staring back at him. He looked alright, not half-bad for just having been nearly flattened by a car; he saw all four paws, his long sleek whiskers, and his thick glowing coat.

Must've just been a trick of the light, he assured himself and flicked his tail, feeling satisfied with the explanation.

Wait... one, two, three, four, five, six, seven... Where's my eighth ring?

He knew he had eight rings on his tail, he'd always had eight rings. He often counted them with the younger kids to help them practice their numbers when they were stuck in bed. Maybe he'd just miscounted...

1 - 2 - 3 - 4 - 5 - 6 - 7 - ?

Still only seven.

An old memory that Desmond didn't even know he had flashed in his mind. *"Had nine of 'em at first. Top one at the tip faded 'bout two weeks ago."*

What had happened that made it disappear? Desmond racked his brain for any memory of his home before the hospital. It was mostly just a blur of warm furry bodies and sweet milk. He remembered he'd had lots of brothers and sisters back then. There had been a black cat, his brother, who had gotten very sick after he was born. Desmond could remember the sound of him wheezing - it sounded like he was trying to breathe underwater.

Desmond saw himself crawling over to the black kitten and laying very close to him. After that he couldn't really remember anything else, except falling asleep. When he woke up the black kitten was breathing perfectly. Was that how he lost his first ring? If it was, then what was the relationship between that time and just 10 minutes ago when he'd lost another.

"Desi, is it true that cats have nine lives?" This simple question hit him like a train. He felt his blood run so cold it felt white hot.

Desmond had been the 9th and final kitten born in a litter. He had been born with 9 rings on his tail. He was now down to 7 and he was almost certain he knew why. Desmond was the only talking cat, as far as *he* knew, at least. Was it possible that talking wasn't the only special thing he could do?

When he was a kitten, he had laid against his sick brother. When they woke, the black kitten was better. That *must* have been when Desmond lost his first ring. Not even twenty minutes ago, he had almost been hit by a car, but miraculously missed it by only inches and again, he'd lost a ring. The second one had to have disappeared in the basement.

Desmond believed it was clear what was happening. Somehow, he could give his lives to others. Somehow, maybe it really was magic, he could transfer his life force to someone else, healing *them*, but shortening his own life. Desmond silently scolded himself for wasting one tonight on something as unimportant as chasing crickets and almost getting killed. That could have gone to a child!

Ollie, he thought.

He knew what he had to do. He didn't know how he was going to do it, but he knew he was going to try. He turned away from the window and ran back down the hall to room 702.

Chapter 22
- The Little Engine that Purred -
(Summer - July 1997)

When Desmond entered Ollie's room it was dark. He could see the shadowy outlines of Mr. and Mrs. Ross slumped against each other in their chairs across the room. They had finally fallen asleep.

Desmond heard the mechanical droning of the machines that were helping Ollie stay alive. He walked slowly to her bed and jumped up without a sound. His paws made soft pitter-patter noises, like falling snow, as he walked up to where Ollie's head rested. Desmond curled himself around the girl's shoulder. He rested his chin in the crook of her collarbone and closed his eyes, letting his purr bubble up thick and slow. The rumbling filled his ears and crashed over him like waves, from the very tips of his whiskers right down to the marrow of his bones. It wasn't long before he drifted off into nothingness.

Chapter 23

- Good Morning -

(Summer - July 1997)

The creeping sun shone over the top of a nearby building, stretching it's light towards Desmond's eyes. It wasn't until the sun blazed fiercely on his face that he finally stirred. His back leg twitched and his front paw jerked up and ruffled his whiskers.

Someone groaned close by. One of Desmond's eyes attempted to open.

"Mmmmm," came the sound again. Even though Desmond was just waking up, he'd never been so tired in his life.

"Ma - mama... dad," it was Ollie. She had woken up with Desmond and the sun.

Exhaustion was weighing on Desmond like heavy stones. It was all he could do to open both eyes at once.

"Gregory! Greg - get up! She's awake!" Desmond felt pressure on his whole body as Ollie's mom leaned over him, or *on* him really, to hug her groggy daughter. The pressure increased and Desmond was sure that Ollie's dad had joined the pile-up.

What happened? the cat thought to himself. He had lain down with Ollie and fallen asleep. Somehow, they had *both* woken up. Desmond couldn't remember exactly what he had done to make Ollie better. The next thing he knew, the morning sun was hot on his fur again. Dr. Clement had walked in and Mr. and Mrs. Ross had disentangled themselves to practically tackle the man in an ecstatic embrace. A chorus of 'thank you!' and 'it's a miracle!' broke out around Desmond and Ollie. When the cat managed to look up, Ollie was staring at him hazily with a mixture of confusion and amazement.

This stare, however, was interrupted - Dr. Clement began shining a flashlight in Ollie's eyes, asking her to follow his finger as he moved it side to side.

"Wiggle your fingers... good! Squeeze my hand... very good... Now wiggle your toes - excellent, kiddo!"

Nobody seemed to notice the silver cat slumped lazily on Ollie's shoulder. All Desmond could think of was how badly he needed to sleep. He knew he would not be able to get the rest he required in here. There was too much excitement; several nurses had come in the room to tell Ollie how spectacular and brave she was.

For her part, Ollie was quiet and had gone back to curiously looking at Desmond. Getting shakily to his feet, he returned her gaze. He winked (he might have winked both eyes, he was so tired, he couldn't really tell), head butted her once and jumped down.

His legs almost gave out from under him when he hit the tile floor and just like that Desmond had left the room. Nobody saw him go - Dr. Clement was rocking happily on his heels. Mrs. Ross was kissing Ollie's cheeks and forehead rapidly while Mr. Ross was pretending to be very interested in a bee just outside the window so he could blow his nose; the nurses clutched their chests and whispered to each other, saying "I just knew she could do it!"

Curling up on his pile of blankets under the desk at the nurse's station, Desmond wrapped his tail up over his eyes to go to sleep.

Hang on, he thought.

1 - 2 - 3 - 4 - 5 - 6...

Sure enough, Desmond counted only six stormy gray rings on his tail. The stack was another ring shorter than before.

It worked, he thought before he fell into a sleep so deep, he did not wake for nearly three days.

Chapter 24

- A Cat is worth A Thousand Words -

(Summer - August 1997)

Desmond woke just after midnight on Tuesday morning. He was parched an starving. His whole body felt as if it had been hollowed out and emptied, like a jack-c lantern on Halloween.

He stumbled clumsily toward his food and water bowl, trying not to trip over his ow feet.

"There you are Des," gasped Dotty, "we were wondering where you'd gone off tc We checked all the kids' rooms - didn't even think to look in your own bed for ya. I honestl can't remember the last time you slept under there. How long were you in that old spot? Dotty scratched his rear as she talked.

Desmond answered her question by gulping down every drop of water and ever morsel of food. He even licked the bowl clean, something he was always much too prou to do before now.

After he ate, Desmond sat with Dotty for a while. He was very glad that she was th overnight nurse on duty that night, because she kept a special brush in her handbag tc groom his fur whenever the hospital wasn't busy. After the stress and chaos of the pas several days or so, Desmond needed a good stress-reliever, and Dotty did not let him down The coarse bristles reached all the way through his thick fur down to his skin. It felt lik finally scratching where you'd had a cast on for months, but over his entire body at once.

The food, water, and brushing gave Desmond new life. He showered Dotty with kisses, head-butts, and purrs before going off in search of Ollie. After all, he didn't want Dotty to think him unappreciative.

The floor was quiet and dim.

When Desmond turned into room 702 it was unusually dark. The moon was entirely hidden behind a wall of clouds.

"I had a feeling you'd be visiting tonight," Ollie was sitting up in bed and though it was pitch black, the faint glow that hung around Desmond like a full-body halo gave him away. He jumped onto the end of the bed.

Moment of truth, he thought.

"How are you feeling?" the cat asked.

Ollie's expression did not change, but her eyes grew so round and bright, Desmond didn't miss the moon at all in that moment.

"I knew it! Well, I didn't really know, but I had weird feeling you could talk. Especially after I woke up the other day and saw you on my shoulder."

"You had us all pretty scared, kiddo."

"Could you always hear me?" she asked.

"Yes, I could always hear you, but I figured out you couldn't hear me pretty early on."

"But why can I hear you now then?"

"I figured it was something to do with the tumor inside you. I've never met a kid who couldn't hear me before, and that was the only reason I could think why."

"You can talk to other kids? Like other kids that stay here?" she waved her arms around indicating all the other occupied rooms.

"Yep, sure can."

"Woah... so, how did you do it?"

"Do what?"

"I don't know, whatever you did to make me better."

"Why do you think I made you better?"

Desmond thought of his tail decorated now by only six rings.

"I dreamt it. I think. I don't remember when the dreams started, but I dreamt that you were talking to me."

"What was I saying?" Desmond was curious as to what he'd said. He had no memory of that night after he'd fallen asleep, if you could even consider what happened to him to be sleep.

"You don't remember?" Ollie asked in awe. Desmond shook his head.

"Well, I only remember bits and pieces, but I think you said things like 'I'm here' and you said my name a lot. You talked about light, or to stay where it was warm or something. And the only thing that was warm was you on my shoulder. So I tried to stay there, like in bed, and I could feel the sound of your purring going all through my body, my fingers and toes, the top of my head, but especially here."

She put her hand on her chest.

"I felt warm everywhere, and then the next thing I knew I was waking up and it was morning."

Desmond flicked his tail but the rest of him was quite still.

"Did you know you could do that?" Ollie asked.

"Not until that night, I didn't. But I'm sure glad I figured it out."

"Me too, kitty."

Desmond took this opportunity to cross the distance between where he sat at Ollie's knees to where her open arms called for him to join her. They sat together in silence for a long time, Ollie gently petting the cat's head and the cat purring with eyes only half open. They watched as the clouds rolled away and made room for the rising sun.

Chapter 25

- Desmond the Cat -

(Fall - December 2000)

The doctors and staff of Piedmont Pediatric Ward experienced six more miracles in Desmond's lifetime. They were never able to make the connection to the curious silver cat who happened to be around every time one occurred and then disappear in the chaotic excitement that followed. Desmond lived on the 7th floor for three more years, making friends, comforting the children during their stays, and, when necessary, giving one of his lives to a child who otherwise would have died.

A week after Desmond turned 6, a new patient by the name of Harvey Kiyoko arrived on the floor. He had a cold that turned into a sickness so wicked and fierce that it left doctors without any hope for recovery.

But there was Desmond, once again and without fail, rising to meet the needs of the children he called his friends. He spent many of his days stretched out on Harvey's bed soaking up the yellow sun of autumn. The cat would watch Harvey count his football cards and when no one else was in the room Desmond would quiz the boy on his favorite players. At night he slept pressed against Harvey's side, his nearly-bare tail, decorated now with just one lonely ring, laid gently across the boy's stomach.

Despite Desmond's brave efforts to help Harvey, it was not long before the doctors accepted that there was nothing more they could do to help the poor child. They did their best to make him comfortable and hung their heads in sorrow when they were in private.

The following morning brought with it something no one could have expected: Harvey awoke spunky and bright-eyed, blinking up at everyone and rubbing his rosy cheeks. That morning he ate his entire breakfast and not one, not two, but *three* cups of chocolate pudding!

The staff was so busy celebrating another miraculous recovery that they didn't notice when Desmond went missing. They found him, however, after finally remembering to look in his own bed of blankets. He had passed away in his sleep, though no one knew why. No one single ring decorated his tail and it looked strangely naked to those who remembered when there had been eight.

Dr. Clement and Dr. Weston had a statue made of Desmond. It gleamed silver and sat on the top of the nurse's station so he could forever watch over the children that came to stay on the floor.

"Mom? Why's there a kitty cat statue?" children would ask as they passed by.

"I don't know. Let's see what it says." They then would read aloud the words engraved on the plaque below the statue:

DESMOND THE CAT - A HERO TO MANY AND A FRIEND TO ALL

CPSIA information can be obtained
at www.ICGtesting.com
Printed in the USA
BVOW08s0819280317
479616BV00001B/4/P